PHOEBE'S PHARAOH

A NOVELLA

CB SAMET

AVANTSTAR
PUBLISHING

Cover Art: GetCovers

Print ISBN: 978-1-950942-11-4

PRAISE FOR CB SAMET

Four-time award winning author

"This was a terrific book…. The ghost of a pharaoh, treasure in an Egyptian tomb, danger, and romance all combine to make an intriguing story. The characters are great and very well written and the plot is great."

— BOOKSPROUT REVIEWER

"[The author's] prose vacillates skillfully between various registers, expressing sensuality, suspense, and humor, as needed."

— KIRKUS REVIEW (ON ROMANCING THE SPIRIT SERIES BOOKS 1-6)

A ROMANCING THE
SPIRIT NOVELLA

PHŒBE'S
PHAROAH

CB SAMET

CHAPTER 1

*A*fter the museum patrons left, Phoebe walked toward the Egyptian exhibit. Her heels echoed through the silent halls. She found the isolation soothing after a busy day of explaining social and cultural anthropology to museum visitors. Now, she was alone with her ancient artifacts—the museum curator and her relics.

Precious artifacts from several Egyptian dynasties lined the walls within the glass cases. Two mummies rested in intricately decorated coffins and a full granite sarcophagus. The exhibit included pottery, chunks of wall with painted hieroglyphics, fragile pieces of papyrus, and canopic jars from various tombs.

"Your exhibit was a big hit."

Phoebe jumped slightly as the security guard entered the hall.

"Sorry, Miss Montgomery. I didn't mean to startle you."

"It's okay, Ray. You're right. The exhibit's been popular with town locals." Phoebe had high school field trips lined up, as well as students from the local university—Penn State. Today, the visitors had been mostly middle-school children.

The elaborate ancient Egyptian exhibit was on loan to Phoebe from the American Museum of Natural History in New York. "It took me a year, and reaching out to numerous larger museums, to get them to loan all these exhibits to us. Finally, we have the 'Phantoms and Pharaohs' showcase." Phoebe spread her arms wide, even though all the spotlights had been turned off after hours. She'd been especially delighted to assemble this collection, since ancient Egypt was one of her favorite eras to study.

"You should be proud."

"Thanks, Ray."

"I'm going to head back to the security office. Let me know when you're leaving, and I'll let you out." He turned, flashlight in hand, and walked away from the Egyptian exhibit.

A flicker of light caught Phoebe's eye beside the black granite sarcophagus. Was a canopic jar glowing? The jar was a typical flat-based, cream-colored limestone jar from one of the late Egyptian dynasties. The lid had been carved into the shape of a jackal—long ears and narrow snout—representing the god Daumutef.

Phoebe wondered if one of the patrons had brought a glow stick and left it behind—but how had it gotten behind the glass exhibit case? On closer inspection, her initial observation was right—the canopic jar was glowing green, and the color was expanding outward.

The light coalesced outside of the glass case and took

the shape of a bronze-skinned man, who appeared translucent.

Phoebe screamed, stumbled backward, and bumped into the stanchion. The red rope surrounding the sarcophagus buckled, and she tumbled to the floor. As she scrabbled around to look at the apparition, she desperately scooted away from it on her butt, pushing with her feet.

"My apologies," the ghost spoke in a deep, male voice with a British accent. "I didn't mean to startle you. Can you *please* stop screaming?"

Phoebe clamped her hand over her mouth, shaking her head. She tried to regain her composure, even as she stared upward at the ghost of an Egyptian pharaoh.

The apparition had an oblong face and wide eyes. An elaborate headdress stretched from above his eyelids into a rectangle. In the center was the motif of a gold snake in an S shape. A postiche—the traditional fake beard that designated him as sovereign in ancient Egyptian custom —protruded from his round chin. The braided fake beard was painted blue and gold.

"This isn't happening," Phoebe stammered, but blinking didn't make the apparition disappear. "I've been working *really* long hours preparing this exhibit. This is just stress." She hardened her gaze at the ancient Egyptian and shook her finger at him. "You're just a manifestation of stress!"

The ghost gave her a pitying look. "I'm sorry, dear lady, to have frightened you. I may not be of the physical world—but I assure you, I'm real."

A flashlight beam struck Phoebe's face, and she screamed again.

"Miss Montgomery?"

"Ray!" She clutched a hand over her chest and felt the rapid, steady pounding of her heart.

"Sorry. I didn't mean to scare you. I heard a commotion back here. Are you okay?"

"Yes, thank you. I just tripped over the boundary rope."

Ray extended a hand and helped Phoebe to her feet. Judging by the way he had no reaction to the presence of the shimmering, semi-transparent pharaoh standing just five feet away from him, Ray clearly couldn't see the ghost.

"Thank you," Phoebe repeated, smoothing down her skirt and tugging a strand of her blond hair out of her face.

"Are you hurt?"

Just my pride, Phoebe thought.

"No, I'm fine."

"You should file an incident report. If an injury turns up because of your fall, you'll want documentation of that."

"Okay. I'll do that. Thank you, Ray."

He adjusted the belt on his blue uniform and began walking away, back down the hallway.

Phoebe shot a glare at the ghostly pharaoh. "My office —*now*," she hissed.

"Beg your pardon?" Ray asked, turning back toward her.

She forced a smile. "I'm going to head to my office now."

Ray nodded and continued walking away, a whistle and a spring in his step as he strode down the darkened hallway.

PHOEBE MADE quick strides to her office and closed the door behind her the moment the pharaoh was inside. She paced the small space, back and forth, marching in front of her bookcase.

"Amyrtaeus," she eventually murmured.

The ghost gave a delighted smile. "Well done! What gave it away?"

"The canopic jar matches the dynasty you're from—one of the later dynasties. Twenty-sixth through thirty-first. I don't recognize you from any ancient artifacts, and you're one of the few pharaohs who never left a monument."

"Well, when you only rule for six years, it's hard to really establish yourself."

"So," Phoebe shook out her hands, trying to eliminate the tremors. "How does this work? You need something to move on?"

"I beg your pardon?"

"My sister, Gigi, suffered... *ghost attacks*—or whatever this is. She said spirits needed help moving on. You know you've come to the wrong sister, right?"

Had he, though? Phoebe thought of the hardship Gigi had endured growing up, seeing ghosts in a world in which no one else could. No one had believed Gigi—no one except Phoebe. She'd been the only one to *really* listen to Gigi, and come to understand that her sister was a girl with rational thought on her side. Gigi wasn't a rambling psychotic suffering from hallucinations. Nevertheless, Gigi wanted to be rid of ghosts and had found medication that had eventually suppressed her ability to see them.

After everything Phoebe's sister had been through, Phoebe couldn't dump this spirit off on her—and certainly couldn't go to Gigi for help.

"Am I the first ghost you've ever seen?"

"You're my first." Phoebe frowned. "*Ghost*," she added for clarity.

"Well, it is an honor," Amyrtaeus gave a flourishing bow, "and unless your sister is also an expert in ancient Egypt, I do *not* believe I've arrived at the wrong sister."

"So, if you're *really* Amyrtaeus—how is it I understand you? And why do you have a British accent?"

"My canopic jar was stored in the British Museum in London for a hundred years—give or take."

"Ah."

Amyrtaeus looked around her office, inspecting the titles of the books on the shelves and the figures from the invoices on her desk. "You've a pleasant little museum here."

Phoebe's museum *would* seem little to someone who'd spent a century in the British Museum.

She leveled her gaze at him. "You're buttering me up for something." Phoebe slumped down in her desk chair, and her feet instantly thanked her.

She'd been on her feet all day, ensuring the museum ran smoothly during operational hours. She'd been museum curator for just over a year now and had been striving to prove herself. Right now, though, Phoebe just wanted to kick off her shoes and sink her toes into the soft, plush rug she kept beneath her desk. But she couldn't relax until she knew what Amyrtaeus needed in order to move on. She couldn't have him haunting her ancient Egyptian exhibit, 'Pharaohs and Phantoms'.

She'd thought that was just a clever name, but perhaps whoever had come up with the title had known the exhibit was haunted.

Amyrtaeus steepled his translucent fingers. "I would like to be reunited with my wife, Chione. I'm worried that if I cross to the other side without Chione, I won't be able to find her again."

Phoebe felt her defensiveness dissolve. "This is all a twenty-five-hundred-year-old love story?"

Amyrtaeus hesitated. "If I answer yes, does that motivate you to help me find her? Or discourage you?"

Despite Phoebe's own disastrous history of relationships, she'd clung to her romantic ideals. The idea of a man wanting to reunite with his wife—and of him waiting three-thousand years to do so—definitely tugged at her heartstrings. However, Phoebe wouldn't reveal such weakness to a ghost. Besides, how difficult could finding his wife in another museum be?

She sighed and tried to make it sound more like irritation than surrender. "I'll help. I've got access to hundreds of museum databases. I can find who has your wife's canopic jar... But then what? Hopefully, you don't expect me to take your jar there? I can't steal your jar from the current exhibit, because it's only on loan to me. Nor can I steal your wife's jar from another museum." She reached for the water bottle on her desk, taking a sip as she leaned back in her chair.

"Right," Amyrtaeus nodded. "Well, there'll be no theft involved. Her canopic jar is still buried near the Hawara pyramid."

Phoebe sat up, choking on her beverage. "Egypt?! You want me to go on an excavation? I'm not an archeologist!"

"You don't need to be an archeologist, because you have me. I'll help you."

"Since you know where Chione is buried, why can't you find her yourself?"

"All the tombs of the wealthy have wards—symbols carved into the walls that prevent spirits from crossing into them. I can't cross them to go to her, and she can't cross them to come to me."

"You weren't buried together?"

"We didn't die at the same time. I was executed and buried decades before Chione died, hence why she wasn't buried with me." He stroked his fake beard, staring solemnly at the ground.

"But you *do* know where?"

"Precisely."

"And you need someone of flesh and blood to fetch her for you?"

"Yes. If Chione's relic is physically carried beyond the wards, we can be reunited."

"What if she's already moved on and didn't stay as a spirit?"

"Then I'll go in peace—cross over, as you say—knowing at least she isn't trapped and waiting for me."

Even without the love story attached, as a museum

curator, the idea of making a brand-new Egyptian discovery appealed to Phoebe. She wasn't an archeologist, but she didn't have to be one if she had a ghost leading the way. Such a monumental discovery could massively advance her career.

"Okay."

"Okay?"

"I'll help you," Phoebe agreed, feeling an ominous weight to her words.

"Splendid." Amyrtaeus beamed happily.

"Not really," Phoebe frowned. "I only have the contents of this exhibit on loan until the end of the month, which means I only have *you* until the end of the month."

Since she'd been planning an international trip for later this year and she'd been to London before, she had an updated passport. She considered the nightmarish logistics—arranging time off work, securing permission to intrude on an excavation site, booking flights and hotels, and figuring out what to pack.

PHOEBE ROCKED SLIGHTLY in her chair as she thought about Amyrtaeus and his canopic jar. If the pharaoh was going to be reunited with his wife, and his spirit was metaphysically connected to his jar, the jar would have to come with Phoebe to Egypt. If she were caught with the jar, she'd be arrested for theft—and her entire career would be ruined.

Equally horrific was the idea of the jar getting broken in her luggage bag, as oblivious airport personnel tossed it onto the cart on the tarmac. The ancient limestone was as fragile as fine china.

Yet, Phoebe had to figure out a way to make this work. She couldn't have a ghost haunting her museum. She certainly couldn't have Amyrtaeus randomly appearing in front of her, making her seem unstable—or downright crazy—to those who couldn't see him.

She pinched the bridge of her nose. "We have an additional confounding factor. I can't just steal your jar off the exhibit. Not only because I don't have the keys, or the ability to shut off the security camera, but also because I can't help you if I'm in jail." Only the security guards had access to the keys of the display cases, and they monitored and controlled the cameras.

"Would you be able to retrieve something from within the canopic jar and leave the actual jar behind?" Amyrtaeus asked.

The pharaoh's question conjured images of a dried-up organ in his jar. In the case of the jackal-headed jar, representing the god Daumutef, Amyrtaeus' stomach would have been placed inside. Of course, after thousands of years, there'd be no organic material remaining. In addition, the artifact had long since been cleaned by the excavators who'd uncovered it.

But if it didn't contain the physical remains of Amyrtaeus—or, at least, part of him—what *did* the jar contain?

"What's inside?" Phoebe asked.

"An emerald. My wife left it for me when I died."

"I'm certain if there were any valuable gems inside your jar, they'd have long since been removed."

"I assure you, it hasn't been removed. My spirit is

connected to the emerald, not the canopic jar. The gem *is* within the jar—it's just not visible by casual inspection."

Phoebe frowned. "I thought Egyptians believed the window to the soul was the heart? That's why the heart was never jarred like other organs, but left inside the mummified body. How come you're attached to that gemstone, not your corpse?"

Amyrtaeus crossed his arms. "Some *also* believed a person's heart would be weighed in the afterlife by Anubis. If the god found it heavy, from an incorrupt life, it would be fed to the monster Ammit. However, it turns out *some* of our beliefs were incorrect." He sighed. "In any event, the soul isn't attached to any one organ. And in my case, my spirit has latched onto my wife's emerald."

"But how do I remove the emerald?" Phoebe demanded. "I can't go about smashing the jar." She thought about the security cameras that would catch her in the act. Plus, the thought of destroying ancient artifacts soured her stomach.

Amyrtaeus smiled reassuringly. "There's a hidden compartment. I'll tell you how to unlock it."

PHOEBE FINISHED DRINKING her water and forced her nerves into calm submission before she made her way to the small nook of the security room, located behind an unmarked door at the front of the museum.

"Hi, Ray."

Ray set down his triple-stack bacon cheeseburger and smiled. "Miss Montgomery! Are you heading out for the evening?" He stood and brushed crumbs off his shirt.

"Not yet. I'm a little worried that, in my clumsiness, I might have damaged something at the exhibit. I'd like to inspect the display case near the sarcophagus."

"Sure, no problem."

She held up a pair of gloves. "You'll be able to open the case for me?"

Ray turned and started typing on the computer. "Yes. Let me deactivate the alarm for that section of the system."

As he typed, Phoebe glanced at the security camera monitors. Three cameras covered the Egyptian exhibit. Was she going to risk her career for a ghost? But not just *any* ghost. Amyrtaeus was a ghost who'd held out for two-and-a-half thousand years to find a way to reunite with his wife—and he was a ghost who knew the location of a previously undiscovered tomb. If there was one thing her sister's experience had impressed upon Phoebe, it was that spirits needed help moving on.

What if this was the first of many ghosts to come? She groaned inwardly. Phoebe didn't think she could take more than one supernatural experience in a lifetime.

Ray escorted her to the exhibit and unlocked the glass cabinet. When she pulled on a pair of soft cotton gloves, he stepped back to give her space.

With her back to both Ray and the security camera mounted on the wall behind them, Phoebe lifted the jar and removed the lid. Her heart pounded fiercely against her ribs. Empty.

"With one hand pressing the button on the bottom, twist the base counter-clockwise."

Phoebe followed Amyrtaeus' instructions. The base

opened to reveal a tiny secret compartment, within which nestled a stunning twenty-carat emerald. Phoebe's hands shook as she slipped the emerald inside the glove on her left hand and re-sealed the bottom of the jar. She set the jar back down and made a show of inspecting the jackal head atop it. The examination gave Phoebe time to appear thorough, while in reality she was just trying to control her breathing and the heat flaring in her cheeks.

Eventually, Phoebe stepped back and closed the case. "Everything looks fine. Thanks, Ray."

The security guard stepped up and locked the case. "No problem, Miss Montgomery."

She slipped off the gloves and began the walk back to her office, forcing her steps to remain slow and deliberate —resisting the frantic urge to run.

"Miss Montgomery?" Ray suddenly called out to her.

Phoebe froze. "Ray?"

Her voice cracked. She couldn't bring herself to turn around and face him.

Ray asked, "Will you be heading home now?"

"Yes, I'm just grabbing my purse."

"Very good—see you tomorrow."

"Thank you, Ray."

CHAPTER 2

*K*enneth watched Phoebe Montgomery walk into a pool hall. What was she up to? He'd been following the curator ever since the Egyptian exhibit had opened at her mini-museum, waiting for her to take the bait from the pharaoh. She wouldn't pass up the discovery of a lifetime. An undiscovered tomb was the dream of any archeologist, or museum curator, especially when so conveniently handed to them through the spirit of someone who knew the precise location.

Phoebe had packed and driven to Washington, D.C. in such a hurry that Kenneth could only surmise Amyrtaeus had introduced himself and Phoebe had accepted the task almost immediately. Why she'd picked D.C., though, Kenneth didn't understand. Egypt would be next, he assured himself. He needed to be patient and continue watching her from the shadows. She absolutely couldn't know about his involvement, at least not until after she'd gone to Egypt and discovered the tomb. His timing would need to be impeccable, so that she'd make the discovery, and he could confiscate it from her shortly afterward—forcefully if necessary.

This tomb, after all, belonged to him. Amyrtaeus had first revealed himself to Kenneth, so he had a right to claim this tomb for himself.

In addition to all the riches it contained.

"Ozymandias Levine?" A woman's voice called his name.

Oz didn't look up as he took aim at the cue ball, planning its course along the green felt. Normally, if a woman called his name, he'd be more responsive, but something in this woman's perfect pronunciation, not to mention the use of his full name, had him wondering if she were someone of authority. Police or IRS? If it was an agency even more sinister than that, she wouldn't have announced her presence in the first place.

He made his shot and sank the eight ball. His opponent slapped a twenty-dollar bill in his hand and walked to the bar.

Oz turned to the woman in the pool hall—the *only* woman in the pool hall. She certainly wasn't police, not with her blond hair pulled back into a smooth bun, or her stiff posture. She was fit but with just the right curve at her hips and bust. The stranger's navy pencil skirt and ivory silk blouse had her looking more like a young librarian.

"I'm Oz," he said.

The woman extended a hand. "Phoebe Montgomery. I'm the museum curator."

Or a museum curator.

Oz shook her hand gently, feeling the warmth of it and watching the way her smile revealed dimples.

He swallowed. *Crap.* This was TJ Montgomery's little sister? Oz had been checking out her tight body just moments earlier, and now he felt certain he'd violated some sort of 'friend code'.

"You're early. I thought we were meeting tomorrow," Oz said.

"I'm always early. Do you have time to discuss the matter now?"

Her expression remained calm, but the way she twisted her fingers together had him curious as to what would make a museum curator nervous.

No wedding ring.

Shoot. He probably wasn't supposed to notice that, either—not about his friend's little sister.

"Sure. Let's discuss." Oz walked to the bar and ordered a shot of tequila—a smooth Don Julio Blanco.

As the bartender poured the drink, Oz walked back to the pool table and began racking the balls.

"Here?" Phoebe looked around, as if the tiny hole-in-the-wall pool hall might be teeming with international spies.

"Miss Montgomery, nobody here cares about three-thousand-year-old Egyptian artifacts."

Her shoulders eased slightly, though she kept her voice low. "I have firsthand knowledge of the location of an undiscovered tomb. Buried within it are several dozen of Egypt's elite, from around the late 300 B.C. era."

Oz handed Phoebe a pool cue.

She accepted it but gave him a puzzled look.

"*If* I accept this job," Oz responded, "I'm not on the clock yet. So, if you want to discuss your artifact—on my night off, no less—we do it over a game of pool. Can you play?"

"I grew up with four older brothers, Mr. Levine. There's no competitive game I can't play."

"Oz."

"Phoebe."

He grinned. He liked Phoebe and the softness of her name. Like her dimples, the name took the edge off some of her sharper features.

She took the cue ball, lined up her shot, and broke the rack. The balls rolled apart in a respectable distribution.

"This tomb is in Egypt?" Oz took aim and pocketed the six.

"Yes. A few hours south of Cairo, there's a dig near the Hawara pyramid. There's a secret, undiscovered chamber and…"

Oz picked the tequila shot off the bar and handed it to her.

Phoebe downed the shot, handed the empty glass back to him, and—without missing a beat—resumed talking, "…and I'm hoping corpses and buried riches will be there as well."

"Not the Valley of Kings? I thought all things from ancient Egypt were there?"

"The Valley of the Kings is a royal burial ground.

There are many other tombs all over Egypt. The tomb I'm looking for came after most of the well-known Egyptian pharaohs were already buried in the Valley of the Kings."

Oz lined up to take his next shot, listening to her talk excitedly about what she hoped to find in Egypt. He didn't mind her intellectual chatter, but he hoped the tequila would help this woman relax. He shot two more solid balls before missing the third shot.

When Phoebe leaned over the table, she stopped talking so she could concentrate. Oz watched her legs stretch all the way up to the curve of her backside.

He rubbed his neck. He most definitely *shouldn't* go on a week-long international excursion with this woman. She was smart, stylish, and attractive.

And she was TJ's little sister.

PHOEBE TOOK aim at the fifteen.

Amyrtaeus pointed his finger toward one edge of the billiard ball. "Aim here. If this barbarian wants you to prove yourself in a game of billiards before he'll help you, then we'll feed him to the scarabs."

Phoebe made the shot, and the ball rolled straight into the corner pocket. However, she didn't consider Oz a barbarian. In fact, from her brother's description, he was a military patriot.

Clearing her throat, she tried to get the burn from the tequila to recede. She didn't normally do shots of liquor, but she was nervous and didn't want Oz to notice.

As she lined up her next shot, Amyrtaeus again

pointed to the spot on the billiard ball she needed to hit to send it spinning off at the perfect angle.

Phoebe said, "TJ said your parents were from Egypt."

"Yes," Oz nodded. "But that doesn't make me an expert in anything Egyptian."

"That's okay. I'm the expert. I need you to be my navigator. I want to hire you because of your military background, not your cultural origins." One-by-one, she knocked the next few stripes into pockets, and then walked around to set up a shot at the eight ball.

Phoebe hadn't originally thought she'd need protection—not until she'd told her brother, TJ, where she was going. He was aggrieved and demanded that she not go to Egypt alone. At first, she'd accused him of being an overprotective military brother, but when TJ had cited several recent instances of violence in the country, she'd caved.

He'd given her the option take one of her brothers or hire somebody. Phoebe didn't want to take a trip with any of her brothers, who'd all have a slew of questions about her uncharacteristic behavior in dashing off to Egypt. After listening to that excuse, TJ recommended Oz instead.

Oz now stood in her way, crowding her at the pool table and looking down at her. "You're a Caucasian American woman traveling to Egypt. You will need a security detail."

She looked at Oz's large hands, wrapped around the pool cue, and then she followed them up to his muscular biceps, protruding from his t-shirt. Her eyes traveled higher to the sinuous muscles of his neck, and his firm, square jaw. Oz had clearly kept in shape since leaving the Marines.

"I realize that," she agreed. "I want to hire *you* to be my security detail." Her heart beat faster at Oz's uncomfortable proximity.

Must be the tequila.

"I'm just one man."

She glanced at his lips before looking up into Oz's intense, dark eyes. "That's all my budget can afford."

When he took a step back, she could breathe again. Phoebe turned and shot the eight ball.

"You didn't call the pocket," Oz said.

"We weren't playing for anything."

"Weren't we?"

She narrowed her eyes at him. Were they playing to see if he'd agree to go with her to Egypt? Phoebe wasn't so desperate that she needed to rely on such a juvenile decision process. Except, she suspected the game was less about winning or losing, and more about Oz gauging whether or not he wanted to take the job. Was he assessing if he thought he could work with her? Was he interviewing her, rather than her interviewing him?

"We'll play again," Phoebe said. She walked to the bar and ordered another shot. She paid for it and knocked down the drink with the same cool efficiency with which she'd downed the billiard balls.

The first shot of tequila had been to take the edge off how tense she'd felt since first seeing the ghost of a pharaoh. The second was to dull the zinging attraction she felt toward a man she knew very little about.

"No cheating this time," Phoebe told Amyrtaeus in a hushed whisper.

The pharaoh rolled his eyes. "You weren't cheating. You were merely using all the resources at your disposal." He flickered away to hover in one corner.

OZ WATCHED Phoebe break the rack, imagining what it would be like to spend a week with her. She tried to mask her nervousness, but something clearly had TJ's little sister on edge. Couldn't be him. Maybe she was simply overstimulated at the prospect of a valuable find, but this wasn't all excitement. A nervous, dangerous energy lurked beneath the surface.

Two shots into the game, Phoebe fumbled the cue but still made a sloppy shot of the three ball into the corner pocket. She was evidently unaccustomed to two shots of liquor in a single fifteen-minute time span.

"You're not drinking?" she asked.

"I don't drink."

She tilted her head to one side. "Then why come here?"

"Show me a pool hall that doesn't serve alcohol."

"Okay, fair enough." Phoebe shrugged. The last words came out slightly slurred. She took another shot, and the cue ball completely missed its target. She stared at the cue stick in her hands, as though insulted that it had the audacity to defy her.

"Did you eat anything before those drinks?"

"No?" Her answer almost sounded like a question.

"No?"

She screwed up her face. "No."

Although it wasn't her turn, Phoebe lined up to take another shot, looking unsteady.

"Okay. Give me the stick." He eased it out of her hand despite her protesting pout. "Let's get you hydrated."

Oz bought a bottle of water before bidding the bartender good night.

Phoebe gulped the water greedily as Oz escorted her out of the bar.

"Where are we going? I'm not in any shape to drive. I don't really drink much."

"You don't say," he grumbled.

"If we stay inside and I drink some water, I'll be fine in a hour."

"Have you booked a room somewhere?"

"No. I drove into town and came straight to see you. I saw a Holiday Inn that way." Phoebe turned and started to walk away from him, vaguely in the direction in which she'd pointed.

Oz steered her back toward his car. "Yes, okay—but you can't *walk* there."

"Can you drive me?"

"Sure." He helped her into his Explorer and started the engine.

"I don't usually drink."

"Yeah, I got that. Keep drinking your water."

Phoebe fell silent as he drove, and Oz wondered if she felt self-conscious about her behavior.

Try small talk.

"So, what makes you think you can find a tomb nobody else has found?"

Amyrtaeus told me where to find it."

"Amyrtaeus? The pharaoh?"

"Yup."

"Verbally *told* you?"

"Yup."

Oz pulled into the parking lot of the hotel. Phoebe leaned her head against his shoulder and closed her eyes. The empty water bottle fell to the floor at her feet.

Ah, heck.

What was he going to do? Get Phoebe a room, haul her into it, and then leave?

Oz pulled out of the parking lot and drove to his apartment. Once there, he helped Phoebe out of his car and practically carried her up the flight of stairs. He unlocked the door and shoved it open. With Phoebe leaning into him, they entered his apartment side-by-side.

"Thanks for getting me a room," Phoebe said, her voice both tired and sultry.

"You might not thank me in the morning."

She might be furious he'd taken her to his place, but it seemed better than dumping TJ's younger sister in a hotel room.

He considered his present options. Couch or bed? No, not the couch. He was currently re-upholstering it. Oz walked her into the bedroom and eased her onto his bed.

"Don't tell TJ I drank too much."

"Your secret's safe with me." He pulled off her pumps to reveal pink toenails.

Throwing a blanket over her to keep her warm, Oz considered the timeline from when TJ had first called him to when Phoebe had arrived at the pool hall. She must have started driving as soon as Oz had agreed to meet her. No wonder she was exhausted.

But what was so urgent about an Egyptian tomb, buried for two-and-a-half thousand years?

Oz looked down at Phoebe as she slept. He glanced at the remaining room on the queensized bed as he kicked off his shoes. He'd thought his military days of sleeping on hard cots and sandy floors were long behind him, but he couldn't share a bed with a woman he hardly knew— clothed or not.

After showering and brushing his teeth, Oz pulled on his boxers. He grabbed a spare blanket from his closet and made himself a bed on the floor of his living room, leaving Phoebe undisturbed.

CHAPTER 3

*P*hoebe blinked her eyes, prying them open as she rolled over beneath the covers. She found herself in an unfamiliar bed in an unfamiliar room.

Instantly, the events of the previous night rushed through her mind. She remembered everything—the billiards, the tequila, and the pharaoh's apparition. Her gaze wandered around the room. No Amyrtaeus. No Oz.

Flopping onto her back, she stared up at the ceiling. She'd never drunk so much she'd had to have someone drive her home before, much less to *his* home. Too much stress, she guessed. This whole thing with the pharaoh was going to break her in two if she didn't incorporate some stress-relief techniques.

Phoebe glanced around the room again. Oz might not be in *this* room, but he was somewhere in his apartment. Knowing she'd already made quite enough of a nuisance of herself, she didn't want to wake him—but she *did* need to use the bathroom.

She eased herself out of bed and tiptoed across the

room. She peeked out of the bedroom to see Oz sleeping on the floor. At first glance, the living room looked to be in bachelor-style disarray, but she soon realized only the couch was a mess. It appeared Oz was applying new upholstery. No wonder he hadn't deposited her on his couch. Noting this, Phoebe then spotted that the bathroom was across the hall from the bedroom.

When Oz rolled over, she ducked back into his room. Phoebe listened carefully, but heard no further movement. She released a slow breath as she crossed the hallway into the bathroom, closing the door behind her.

After she'd finished in the bathroom and taken a quick minute to freshen up, she eased the door back open. Oz, she could see, was still sleeping. On her tiptoes once again, Phoebe crept around his bedroom until she located her shoes. She picked them up and left the bedroom.

Was Oz a furniture maker? Her brother said they'd served in the Marines together and then Oz had gone into some type of special operations section. According to TJ, Oz had recently left the Marines and was currently between jobs. Her brother had told her Oz was 'getting his civilian legs back under him.' Was that a thing? She had no doubt soldiers needed a certain amount of time to re-acclimate to a civilian lifestyle.

Now, Oz played pool—sober pool, on a Friday night— and reupholstered his own couch. Okay, maybe Phoebe could envision that lifestyle for him. After all, he seemed at ease.

Oz also seemed like a decent human being. And a rational one. Not the sort of person who'd follow Phoebe to Egypt if she claimed she was taking orders from the ghost of a pharaoh. Oz would probably drive her directly to the nearest psychiatric ward if she shared such 'hallucinations' with him. Heck, she'd been tempted to drive herself there a few times over the last day.

Except Phoebe knew this wasn't a hallucination. She knew because her sister had been able to see ghosts, too. Phoebe was the only person Gigi trusted with knowledge of her visions. Mild sedatives seemed to have severed the connection and eased her sister's tortured anxiety. As a result of taking them, Gigi hadn't seen any ghosts in years, at least, none that she'd confided to Phoebe. Gigi would have been a great resource for Phoebe to turn to now, but she didn't want to stir painful memories for her little sister, especially since Gigi had worked so hard to suppress them.

Besides, the task seemed simple enough: travel to Cairo, locate the tomb, and free Amyrtaeus to move from this dimension to the spirit world. Then, Phoebe could be rid of the spirit and not suffer nervous breakdowns the way Gigi had.

Between paying for the trip and paying for an additional traveler, however, Phoebe suspected she'd have to use the money she'd been saving for her first real vacation. She wasn't talking about the brief weekend beach trips she'd taken during college, but a week-long trip to Europe—perhaps to Paris, or Rome, or Alsace. Now, she'd have to start saving from scratch again.

Phoebe spotted her purse on the counter. Beside it lay her phone, which was plugged into a charger she could only assume belonged to Oz. She was impressed. Only a *really* decent man would think to charge a woman's phone for her.

Now what?

She couldn't walk back to get her car. She wasn't even sure where that was from here. Instead, Phoebe picked up her phone, selected an app, and began typing. Since she wasn't going to be able to sneak away from Oz's apartment, like a kid sneaking out of the house, she'd have to own up to her sophomoric behavior last night.

Using the map on her phone, she found the nearest coffee shop using a quarter of a mile away. She could walk there, pick up coffee for the both of them, and return like a mature adult who hadn't excessively consumed tequila last night.

Oz HEARD the door to his apartment close. He sat up and scrubbed his hands over his face. Where was Phoebe going? And on foot?

He threw off the covers, walked to the bathroom, and cleaned up.

He'd only been pretending to be asleep for part of this time. He'd detected Phoebe stealthily moving around his bedroom, the same way a woman does when she slinks away after a one-night stand. She was obviously embarrassed to have woken up in his bed. Because Phoebe had been trying so hard not to wake him, Oz had opted to pretend to continue to sleep so as not to disappoint her. Still, he found the conceit amusing. Did Phoebe honestly think she could covertly sneak out of the room of a Marine?

Retired-Marine, Oz.

With that thought, his right shoulder began to ache. He ran through a series of stretches and exercises he'd learned during physical therapy.

He needed to remember he was a civilian now—and he needed to find a job. That thought had him wanting to check his email. He'd been waiting to hear back from a place he'd applied to ten days ago. Typically, Oz only checked his email two or three times a day, but today was Saturday.

Cool your gears.

There wouldn't be any news for at least two days. *If* he'd got the job and *if* they notified him Monday, it would probably still be a few weeks before they wanted an interview, background checks and all.

So, that meant he almost certainly had a week to join Phoebe in Egypt, should he decide to do so. Or rather, if she still wanted him, since she'd snuck out in a manner suggesting she might not be back. Phoebe could have gone outside and caught a rideshare, which might mean he'd never see her again.

Oz dismissed the thought. She'd clearly been too keen on hiring him yesterday to back out because of a simple mishap, for which he certainly didn't judge her. He thought once again about the nervous intertwining of her long, delicate fingers. Phoebe clearly needed to go to Egypt, but something about the trip—or the prospect of the find—had her both excited and afraid.

Why would a trip to a tomb be dangerous? Did she want a former military man to escort her because she feared being in a foreign country? Or was it something else?

When TJ had first called Oz, he'd explained that he'd coerced his sister into recruiting a companion for safety. TJ had picked Oz because he'd felt him trustworthy, not because he'd imagined Phoebe needed Oz's military skillset. Yet, Phoebe had acted in a nervous manner, suggesting she thought she might need *actual* protection.

Oz pulled on a pair of blue jeans and walked back into his living room. He could work on his couch until Phoebe called, and she *would* call. For starters, she wouldn't make it more than a mile walking in those shoes.

His phone rang. He fetched the phone from his nightstand. It was the other Montgomery—TJ.

"Montgomery! What can I do for you?"

"Hey, Ozy. You're probably meeting with my sister today, and I appreciate you taking the time. I just wanted to warn you that she can be a little... *uptight*."

"I met her."

"Already?"

"She arrived last night. She told me over a game of pool what she's looking for."

"Last night? That's got to be some kind of record travel time."

"I guess you can't keep a museum curator from the prospect of finding ancient artifacts."

"You two played billiards?" TJ's tone sounded baffled rather than overprotective.

"Yeah, she beat me." True to his promise, Oz wouldn't mention Phoebe's drinking.

"Are you going to take the job?"

"We've got more to discuss."

"She's there with you now?"

Oz bit his lip, feeling a bit mischievous. "She spent the night last night."

"*What?*"

Oz kept himself from outright laughing at his friend, but his misleading statement also confirmed Oz's suspicion that he should keep his hands *off* Montgomery's sister.

"Okay, relax, Marine. Nothing happened. She got in late and needed somewhere to crash."

"If you take this job, it does *not* include cozying up to my little sister."

"Pipe down. If I take this job, it'll be to repay you. Why is she single anyway?"

"Probably because she's more interested in mummies than men."

Oz chuckled.

"I dunno," TJ continued. "I think she was serious about some older man a while back, but he cheated on her or something. She talks to our sister about these things, not me."

"Noted."

"Thanks for meeting with her. She seems to think this is important and time-sensitive. How that's possible with something that's been underground for nearly three millennia, is a mystery to me."

"I'll look after her."

"Thanks, Ozzy. Hey, how's the job search going?"

"Going well. I'm trying to get a cryptology position."

"Huh."

"Huh, what?"

"Well, it sounds cool—it just doesn't sound like you. I don't picture you working a desk job, but then again, when we first met, neither of us were desk jockeys."

TJ knew that after their military careers had split on different paths, Oz had gone on to join the MARSOC special operations unit of the Marines. Oz had traveled extensively with the job, performing special reconnaissance, foreign internal defense, and counter-terrorism operations. "Well, when a bullet to the shoulder incapacitates your ability to raise an M16, it's time for a desk job."

"Don't ever stop reminding yourself you're a hero, *and* you're lucky to be alive."

Since Oz had been on a covert operation at the time, TJ had no idea about the nature of the mission in which Oz had been injured, but he was right about the 'lucky to be alive' thing. Alive *and* functional.

Oz thought of a fragment of the MARSOC Critical Skills Operator creed:

> *I will never quit,*
> *I will never surrender,*
> *I will never fail.*

Unless I get injured. Then, I'm honorably discharged and left making a career change.

But an honorable discharge wasn't quitting, or surrendering, or failing—and Oz was ready for a change.

"Anyway, good luck with your new job," TJ added,

"and thanks again for looking after my sister. Consider us even for Tajikistan."

"Thanks."

~

THE FRESH AIR felt good on Phoebe's face as she walked along the sidewalk toward the coffee shop.

Amyrtaeus appeared beside her. "Do you think Officer Levine will take the job?"

Phoebe gasped, startled. She wasn't sure if she'd ever acclimate to having a ghost appear on a whim beside her. Hopefully, if this trip to Egypt worked out, she wouldn't have to.

Then she focused on Amyrtaeus' words.

Officer?

Had Oz been an officer in the Marine Corps? She hadn't got many robust details about him from her brother. TJ had told her Oz and he had been in the Marines together and that Oz "owed him one."

"Maybe we can work on a system in which you *dissolve* into sight—slowly. If I keep jumping out of my skin every time you appear, Oz is going to think I'm crazy. He may already think that. Anyway, no—he's not agreed yet."

"Offer him more money."

"I'm not a pharaoh with access to unlimited gold and riches."

"You will be," Amyrtaeus grinned.

"Whatever we find in Egypt will belong to the Egyptian government. I'm not a grave robber."

"If you're not doing it for the money, why do it?"

"You need to move on, for one. I can't have you hovering around me for the rest of my life. For two, you want to be reunited with your wife. Who can say no to that? And lastly, this will be a great archaeological find. A little publicity might put my humble museum on the map."

"Ah, notoriety, yes. Did you know the sphinx of my successor—Nepherites the First—is in the Louvre museum?"

"I *did* know that."

"Know it all." He waved an annoyed hand at her.

"What's your rush about making your way to your wife's tomb? You've made this entire thing seem very urgent, and it's escalating my anxiety."

"If you don't find it before you have to return the exhibit, I'll have to wait until my exhibit lands with another medium."

Phoebe nodded as she walked along the sidewalk. "I have your emerald now. I can keep it longer, even if the exhibit goes back. Nobody else knows about it."

"…and," Amyrtaeus continued, "someone *else* is after the tomb, and the fortune it contains. A rather dubious gentleman once tried to goad the location out of me a few years ago. He oozed greed. I didn't trust him."

"What does it matter to you who finds it, as long as it's found?"

"I'd like a person with a certain moral caliber to partake in the discovery. One careless, selfish move and I might never see my wife again."

"Okay, but that still doesn't explain the urgency. This

dubious character doesn't have *you*, so he can't find the tomb, right?"

"Right," Amyrtaeus' agreement came out in a disgruntled tone, "and yet, *something* feels urgent about it."

"A sixth sense?" Phoebe teased.

"An angst."

"Well, stop transferring your angst onto me. I have enough on my own plate—what with seeing a ghost and orchestrating an archeological find." She reached for the doorknob of the coffee shop. "Now shoo, so I'm not seen talking to myself."

Amyrtaeus vanished.

Oz set his phone down and walked into his kitchen to fix a pot of coffee.

"Knock? Knock?" Phoebe walked back in through the front door to his apartment, carrying two cups of coffee and a paper bag. She bumped the door shut with her hip.

Oz stared at her for a moment, mesmerized by the motion of her waist. When his eyes met hers, he could tell she was staring at him the same way he'd been staring at her.

"I brought... " She blinked several times. "I brought coffee. And bagels. Coffee *and* bagels." She cleared her throat as she handed Oz one of the coffees, and then looked sharply away, seemingly to avoid eye contact.

Still looking away, she set the bag with the bagels down on the counter. "I didn't know how you like your coffee, so it's black, but there's cream and sugar in the bag."

"Black is perfect."

Phoebe pulled the lid off her cup, blew on the steam, and took a sip.

"Do you want to talk more about the job?" he asked.

"Yes." She turned toward him with flushed cheeks. "Can you put a shirt on?"

Oz looked down. "Oh, right. Sure." He walked into his bedroom and pulled on a t-shirt.

Into mummies more than men, TJ? I don't think so.

But as he dressed, Oz wondered what would make Phoebe so flustered by the absence of his shirt? Oz thought about Montgomery's comment about the man who'd cheated on her. TJ said it had happened years ago. Had she not been with anyone else since then? Surely, she wouldn't let one jerk deter her from all future relationships.

In any case, none of that was Oz's business. He needed to learn more about what the trip to Egypt entailed.

As he walked back into the living room and toward his coffee, he opened his arms wide. "I'm decent. You want to tell me about Egypt now?" He leaned on the kitchen counter, sipping his coffee.

"There was once a pharaoh who ruled for five years, back in the twenty-eighth dynasty." Phoebe hesitated as if interrupted. "Five-and-a-*half* years, sorry. His name was Amyrtaeus of Sais. He's not well known and didn't leave any monuments. There *is* a tomb with treasure in it, which is related to him tangentially."

"What makes you think you can find this tomb? When

thousands of archeologists have combed Egypt for relics for hundreds of years?"

She bristled.

"No offense intended," Oz added, "but you seem very eager, like a woman with a secret password to a secret club."

"I've been studying the Demotic Chronicles and…"

"Demonic. That sounds ominous."

"De-mo-*tic*. It's Egyptian text chronicling the twenty-eighth, twenty-ninth, and thirtieth dynasties."

"Only three?"

"Three important ones. Three during the independence interval."

"Independence from whom?"

"The Persians. Do you know any Egyptian history?"

"I was born and raised in New Jersey."

"But your parents…"

"Fled during the Revolution of 1952. Their parents were sympathizers to King Farouh and wealthy landowners. They took their wealth, left their land, and never went home. Modern Egypt, I know. Ancient Egypt, I don't."

Phoebe smiled. "Then we're a perfect fit. I know ancient Egypt but not modern Egypt."

Her words "perfect fit" had Oz thinking of their proximity while he'd considered sleeping beside her on the bed last night, and the way she'd leaned over the pool table. Were they a perfect fit?

Oz shook his head. He'd never find out, because he'd never make a move on TJ's little sister.

"So, don't you need some type of government permission to go exploring in another country?"

"Already arranged. I've got a colleague from the University of Alabama. She's cleared me to join their group. UAB archeologists are part of the team who discovered over eight hundred tombs in Lisht in 2018. It was an enormous find."

"Lisht."

"It's a village south of Cairo, where the Middle Kingdom's royal and elite were buried."

Oz nodded. "I know the geography. Is that where Amyrtaeus' tomb is?"

"No. The Lisht part was just to impress you—that an archeologist friend of mine was part of the discovery of the century. But I can see you're less than silenced with awe and fascinated wonder."

"No, no! It's very impressive. Don't be discouraged by my contemplation. I just like to see logic and patterns in everything."

"Okay, so, I have information about where I might find an undiscovered treasure, so logically I want to make the historic find."

"But you're not an archeologist."

"I'm not."

"So, why not let your colleague know where to find it? Why travel all the way to Egypt if a team is already there? You don't strike me as the Indiana Jones 'fortune and glory' type."

Phoebe glanced in the direction of his living room window—as if someone was standing there—before she looked back and gave a sheepish grin. "Because: 'It belongs in a museum?'"

Oz released a hearty laugh. Phoebe was startled at first and then laughed with him.

Even in the relaxed moment, Oz felt a knot of tension. There was no *way* he should take an international trip with this delightful woman. "When do we leave?"

CHAPTER 4

*P*hoebe rented a hotel room in Washington, D.C. later that day and then spent three days preparing for the upcoming trip. She used her laptop to book flights and hotels. She'd already packed clothes for the trip, but now she had time to consider all the additional items they would need. She bought flashlights, face masks, glow sticks, and water canteens.

She carefully arranged the contents in her luggage.

"You are quite prepared, I believe," Amyrtaeus said, dissolving in slowly beside her, so as not to startle her.

"I hope so. I'll probably still look like an amateur to Oz."

"I believe, my dear, that everyone looks like an amateur to a man like Officer Levine."

"Why do you say that? And you keep calling him officer. Was he an officer in the Marines?"

"He was in the Marines' Special Operations unit. The best of the best. I liken him to the Medjay from ancient Egypt."

Phoebe stopped packing and stared at the ghost. "An elite paramilitary force with combat skills and espionage training?"

"Yes, Mr. Levine was more like that."

Phoebe felt her mouth go dry. Oz was inordinately overqualified for the role she'd hired him for. This trip must seem like child's play to a man like him.

"Yes, he was quite proficient," Amyrtaeus nodded. "In Mr. Levine's case, there was this one instance in the Czech Republic…"

"Don't tell me that!" she snapped. "That's probably a government secret even he can't talk about. How do you know that anyway?"

"Ghosts can glean bits and pieces of people's past— and, occasionally, their future."

"But he's retired."

"Honorably discharged following an injury."

Special Operations? Phoebe resumed packing. Why would someone of Oz's caliber take up Phoebe's humble offer to be hired muscle, and travel with her to Egypt? Her brother must have cashed in a big favor. Did TJ know about Oz's career in Special Operations?

"Have you gleaned pieces of *my* past?" Phoebe partially closed the bathroom door and changed into her pajamas beyond the eyes of Amyrtaeus.

"Fragments. A happy childhood. The usual sibling rivalry. Supportive parents. Mr. Levine, on the other hand…"

"No, no. If there's something in his past he wants to share with me, that's *his* decision. Your telling me about him is like spying." Phoebe crawled into bed.

Amyrtaeus stood near the window. "Well, he's an honorable man. Perhaps the challenges of his formative years made him into the man he is today."

Phoebe fluffed her pillow before lying on her back and staring up at the ceiling. "Tell me about your wife."

"Her name was Chione. It means *daughter of the Nile.* She had long black hair—about the length of yours. Her eyes were large and brown, and positively radiant when she smiled. She loved the lotus flower, watching raindrops dance on the river's surface, and the smell of fresh papyrus."

"How did you meet?"

"Oh, it was all prearranged back then. Marriage was a business, and rational parents made the arrangements. We didn't have elaborate ceremonies. I see the benefit to both love-driven relationships and business relationships—but people can *learn* to love, especially when parents choose someone of similar class and interests."

"Sounds sterile."

Amyrtaeus laughed. "Ah—and what do modern-day suitors do? Hmm? Don't they click-click-click on the internet? Use services programmed to find compatible partners by means of shared interests, hobbies, and careers? Is that so different? Is that any less *sterile?*"

Phoebe chuckled. "Okay. Point taken." Who knew a three-thousand-year-old pharaoh would have the insight to identify similarities in human culture that spanned millennia?

"What about you and Mr. Levine?"

"Oh, no! We were talking about you and Chione. Don't turn this on me."

"You two seem compatible—and there's chemistry…" Amyrtaeus' voice trailed.

"There is?" She didn't like the hopeful tone in her voice.

Dang, Amyrtaeus had baited her into talking about Oz.

"Never mind. We're *not* discussing this. I need sleep." Phoebe reached over and turned out the light.

"Good night, Miss Montgomery."

OZ CLIPPED on his seat belt as he sat beside Phoebe on the plane. He'd been amazed to learn she'd driven to DC almost fully packed for an international trip. She'd either been highly confident that Oz would join her—or determined enough to go with or without him, regardless of his decision. Based on Phoebe's sense of urgency, he suspected the latter.

"Business class is nice," he commented.

Phoebe slid her shoulder bag under the seat. She wore jeans and a pink blouse. The look was more relaxed compared to when he'd first met her, though her hair was still pulled sharply back and up.

"I thought you could use the extra leg room," Phoebe explained. "It's not first class, but it's more comfortable than cattle class for an overseas flight. First class is out of my budget. Otherwise, I'd have shown my gratitude with a fully reclining chair."

"I've taken numerous international flights in worse than cattle class, as you call it, so this is a nice step up. Consider your gratitude expressed."

"Travel trips? For business or pleasure?"

"Business."

"TJ said you retired from the Marines. Must be good to have the stress of that behind you."

"Bitter sweet. Sometimes I miss it."

"What are your plans now that you're done? Aside from re-upholstering furniture and taking impromptu civilian security details?" She crossed her legs.

He rubbed his hands on his blue jeans. He had a plan, but he needed to get the position he'd applied for first. "I'm applying for a cryptography position."

"Oh, very cool. What type of training does that involve?"

"I have a master's degree in cybersecurity thanks to Uncle Sam."

"Sounds intense."

"No more intense than an undergraduate history and art dual major, followed by a doctorate in museum studies."

"Oh, you've looked me up. Well, you should know my family accused me of being a professional student at one point."

"I wouldn't travel with anyone I hadn't researched. And you finished all of those degrees in a condensed time, so don't discredit yourself... or let your family do so."

"Well, it's no special operations."

Oz cocked his head to one side. "TJ tell you that?"

A flicker of concern crossed her face before she forced a smile. "I have my sources."

TJ might have known Oz was Special Operations, but he was unlikely to share that information with anyone.

Oz had never explicitly told TJ what role he'd moved onto after they served their first three years together. If TJ wasn't her source, who was?

Oz watched the gentle bob of Phoebe's throat as she pulled out a magazine to browse. She'd clearly realized she'd divulged knowledge she wasn't supposed to have.

He would find out who her source was. Not on a plane full of people, but soon.

PHOEBE WALKED beside Oz as they stretched their legs. The flight from Dulles to Abu Dhabi had been just over fifteen hours.

She took the plastic lid off the top of her coffee and slowly sipped the warm liquid, feeling its revitalizing power.

"I noticed you always do that with your coffee—take the lid off. You know they put that hole in the lid for you to drink through?" Oz demonstrated by drinking his own coffee with the lid still in place.

She chuckled. "Yes, I'm aware. I have this aversion to drinking that way. It's always felt like a sippy-cup when I drink with the lid on."

He grinned and took a sip with his lid firmly in place. "I guess I'm embracing my inner child."

"No, I don't judge anyone else. I know it's my own quirk."

They took seats beside each other in the terminal as they waited for their next flight.

"I have to ask," he began. "Why not bring your boyfriend or TJ on this trip? Why hire a stranger?"

"I don't have a boyfriend, and my brother—actually *brothers*, any one of them—would pester me."

"No boyfriend? Is that because you work too much? It's okay. Sometimes people get wedded to their work. I didn't date much during my last job."

Phoebe suspected the reason was as much the nature of Oz's work as the time he'd spent performing it.

"I have trust issues." As soon as she blurted out the confession, she wished she could take it back. A man like Oz wouldn't let such a detail-free statement serve as a satisfactory explanation.

"Lots of people have trust issues. That doesn't prohibit dating."

"I dated a married man." She cringed at her own words.

"I take it that didn't end well."

"I didn't know he was married. I should have, but I didn't."

Oz raised an eyebrow. "*He* knew, though." His tone sounded curious rather than judgmental.

"Uh, well, yes—and it gets worse."

"Does it?" He took another sip of his coffee.

"He was my college professor. I was twenty, and he was forty. Forty *and* married. He taught art history. He's the reason I fell in love with Egyptian art. Anyway, I was young and stupid, and he cheated on his wife because of me. For three months."

"A whole three months?"

She elbowed Oz lightly in the arm. "Don't make fun."

Truthfully, the way Oz simply listened made it easy to share her tale, and it was almost cathartic to confess her past to him.

He reassured her, "He didn't cheat *because* of you. He cheated on his wife because he's a scumbag. You can't blame yourself for that."

"Thanks."

"Now, back to the part about you sleeping with a man twice your age." Oz shook his head. "*That's* on you."

She turned her nose up at him. "Anyway, as soon as I found out—as soon as one of my classmates pointed out he was married—I confronted him."

"Good for you. How'd that go?"

"He said: Of course he was married—despite never wearing his ring—and not to worry, because I'd earn an 'A' in his class. We hadn't even taken final exams yet. I felt so cheap, like I'd traded sex for grades."

Oz's jaw tensed. "What'd you do?"

"I stayed in the class and earned my own darn 'A'—all while nursing what I'd thought was a broken heart."

"You don't think it was broken?"

"It wasn't love. It was infatuation. That involves lust, not love. If the heart was never truly involved, then it couldn't have been broken."

Oz rubbed his chin. "Sounds logical."

"What?"

He hesitated before asking, "That's the last guy you've been with? Eight years ago?"

Phoebe felt heat creep from her neck into her cheeks. "I've dated." The defensive tone in her own voice irritated her.

She'd dated but never lost herself in a relationship since then. She'd never trusted her own emotions enough to turn them loose and indulge in a romantic relationship. She'd been called stiff, aloof, and probably worse. One man she'd dated had accused her of setting her standards too high—higher than any man could achieve. She'd never given him any set of standards to meet; she just hadn't been willing to sleep with him, as if flowers and chocolates were supposed to make her crawl into his bed.

Trust.

That's what had been missing.

She'd never found unwavering *trust* in a man—and maybe she'd never completely trusted herself, either. She'd poured out her hopes and dreams, and everything else about her and her family to a man who'd used her and sent her on her way.

But was it trust that had made her tell Oz her dirty, shameful secret? A secret that suddenly didn't feel so dirty or shameful anymore?

Oz shifted his weight in the airport chair. "Your professor shouldn't have said that about your grade. He shouldn't have made you feel cheap. I hope you've come to recognize he's a jerk."

"Yes. Yes, I have."

PHOEBE FELT wobbly after they left the plane. She hadn't slept well on the flight. Instead, she'd watched Oz sleep like a baby—his long legs extended, sinewy arms crossed, and his dark eyes closed.

Now that they'd arrived in Cairo, Phoebe tossed her bags over one shoulder and followed Oz through the terminal to the baggage claim. While she waited at the concourse, she checked work email on her phone. No crisis at the museum. A kid had been caught sticking gum to one of the Ming dynasty Chinese vases, but that had been the extent of the excitement.

She hated missing even one day of her prize exhibit being showcased, but circumstances being what they were, she'd had to go to Egypt. Amyrtaeus needed to fully cross over to the spirit world, and Phoebe had a chance to make an amazing discovery by finding this tomb.

She'd gone over the details of the tunnel and tomb with Amyrtaeus, although she had the distinct impression he'd forgotten many of the details. Phoebe hoped once they were physically *in* the passageways, he would remember more.

"Are you okay?" Oz asked. He was by her side, holding her elbow.

Phoebe looked down at where he'd touched her, and then back up at him. She was surprised to see his expression of concern.

"I'm fine."

"You were teetering."

"I don't teeter."

"You haven't eaten, and you looked unsteady."

"I'm okay. I don't like to eat much when I travel, and I did eat while you were asleep, thank you very much."

He narrowed his eyes at her. "That was a protein bar. That's not enough for a mouse over a twelve-hour period."

"I'm probably just dehydrated."

Oz released her elbow, reached into her bag, and pulled out her water bottle.

She accepted it. "You're taking this protection detail a bit far, don't you think?"

"Sometimes people need protection from themselves and their poor decisions."

Poor decisions.

Phoebe looked away. His words conjured images of her affair with her professor. Yes, people *did* need protection from themselves.

Eight years, Phoebe. Let it go.

As she drank the water, Oz walked away and retrieved their luggage. When he returned, she dropped the bottle back in the bag and took her rolling suitcase from him.

"All better." She smiled. "Taxi?"

"Taxi."

"WE'RE HERE TO CHECK IN," Oz said at the reception desk. "Reservations for two rooms—Montgomery and Levine."

The hotel clerk typed in the names with an unwavering smile on his face. His nametag read Omar. Then, Omar's face suddenly fell. He picked up the phone and began speaking in Arabic to the person on the other end of the line.

When Omar finally hung up the phone, he pulled his expression back into a smile. "Ms. Montgomery, I am *very* sorry, but your room is having plumbing problems. I want to move you to another room, but it will have to be when the next guest checks out."

"How long will that be?" Phoebe asked.

"Just a few hours. You could have dinner and come back?"

Oz looked at Phoebe, who'd probably only slept a few hours in the last day. "Take my room. I'll wait for the next one."

"Really? No, I don't want to do that to you... *again*."

Omar leaned forward on the counter. "It has a king-size bed."

Oz wriggled his eyebrows at her from an angle the clerk couldn't see.

She laughed. "I would like to lie down for a little while."

After they received the key, the two of them took the elevator to the fifth floor and found the room.

Oz inspected the hotel room, not because he anticipated danger, but out of force of habit. The room was modern, with a nice frieze of golden pyramids along the wall behind a king-sized bed with crisp, blue linen. From the balcony of the room, he could see the Nile River.

"I'm going to take a walk and let you catch some zzzz's."

CHAPTER 5

*P*hoebe unpacked a few things and then went to the bathroom to begin brushing her teeth. "You can rest here. You don't have to wait in the bar or lounge."

Oz was inspecting the room so thoroughly, she imagined even a cockroach couldn't escape his sharp eyes. Was he worried about security at the hotel? She'd hired him more for the protection detail traveling around Egypt. She wasn't expecting any danger at the hotel. In fact, only her museum staff, TJ, and her archeologist friend knew she'd even come to Egypt in the first place.

"I'll let you rest," Oz said.

"I'm a heavy sleeper, excluding planes."

Oz plucked his backpack off the floor and left the room. Phoebe sighed. Once again, she'd invaded his space.

"Ah, Egypt."Amyrtaeus appeared, and Phoebe nearly jumped out of her skin.

He'd been pleasantly *not* lurking about for the last

several days while they traveled to Egypt—but now, apparently, the pharaoh was back.

He took a deep breath. "What does it smell like?"

She grinned mischievously as her voice turned wistful. "Like roasted duck with a side of garlic-smothered lentils and bread infused with honey and dates. Like the fresh water of the Nile has suffused the air after a heavy rain. Like the blooming of a garden rich with mandrakes, jasmine, and roses."

"Really?"

"No. It smells like a hotel room."

Amyrtaeus chuckled.

Phoebe crawled under the covers and closed her eyes. "Goodnight, Amyrtaeus."

"Goodnight, Miss Montgomery."

PHOEBE HELD her flashlight high as she looked around the chamber. The walls were rustic, made from clay covered in vibrantly painted hieroglyphics: a vulture for 'A', a hand for 'D', a ripple of water for 'N'. A conglomeration of symbols formed the words 'day' and 'night' above a drawing of the sun god, Ra.

The air in the tomb was dry, and Phoebe blinked through a gritty sensation in her eyes. In the center of the room, a black stone sarcophagus rested. She walked closer to inspect the carvings. An ankh was carved into the stone, representing the key to the gates of death, and what lay beyond.

When she was a foot away from the sarcophagus, she

stepped on something more rigid than the layer of sand on the stone flooring. It sank into the ground beneath her weight. Looking down, she gaped at what appeared to be a pressure-sensitive brick the size of a man's fist. A bone-chilling, grinding noise reverberated throughout the chamber.

Frozen in astonishment, she watched the stone sarcophagus begin lowering into the ground. The walls all around her shook. She took a step away from the descending sarcophagus when someone roughly shoved her from behind. Stumbling forward, she fell into the sarcophagus.

She landed on her side with a thud. As she tried desperately to scramble to her feet, sand began rapidly filling the space around her—and *over* her! In a panic, she thrashed widely, as the light of her flashlight swirling like a strobe light.

When the sand covered the flashlight, the coffin went dark.

Phoebe screamed.

Large warm arms wrapped around her. "Shh! Phoebe. It's okay. You had a bad dream."

She stilled her thrashing, her heart thudding like it would beat right out of her chest at any moment.

"You're okay," Oz said in a soothing voice.

The warmth of his embrace calmed her until, at last, Phoebe's breathing slowed to normal.

Faint morning light streamed in through the window. Blinking, she recognized the hotel room. They'd only just arrived, she remembered. She hadn't been to any tombs yet. What had started as a nap must have turned into an overnight slumber.

Oz still held her from behind, but he'd relaxed his hold.

"I'm sorry. I'm okay." Mortified, Phoebe eased away from him—from the smell of cinnamon and cedar, the security of his embrace, and the radiance of his touch.

Was she ever going to be anything but a nuisance to this man?

Without making eye contact with Oz, she clambered out of bed, walked to her suitcase, and retrieved fresh clothes. She took her bundle to the bathroom and changed. There, she splashed water on her face and applied a touch makeup to cover the dark circles under her eyes.

Amyrtaeus dissolved into the room. "I'm sorry about your nightmare. I fear it may be the result of the danger I'm sensing."

"What danger?" Phoebe whispered, her tone grouchy with annoyance.

"I don't know. It's a feeling. Nothing concrete."

"Well, stop projecting your feelings onto me."

"Are you okay?" Oz asked from the other side of the door.

She gave Amyrtaeus a sour look before turning and swinging the door open. "I'm great."

Oz arched a disbelieving eyebrow at her. "What's going on, Phoebe?"

"Why are you in this room?" she asked.

"A family of five with three kids had a flight cancellation and needed to stay another night, so I gave them my room. I napped on the edge of the bed—that is until you started thrashing about."

"Okay." Phoebe smoothed down her pants and walked toward her suitcase to grab her brown boots.

Oz stood up, wearing his standard attire of t-shirt and blue jeans. "Phoebe?"

"Are you ready to start? Maybe grab a bite to eat first? This is an all-expenses-paid trip for you."

"*Phoebe*," he snapped.

She swallowed at the directness of his tone and the intensity of his stare.

"I'm not going anywhere until you tell me what's going on." Oz's voice was quiet and nonthreatening, but firm.

"I had a bad dream. I fell into a sarcophagus, and I was being buried alive." She picked up a long boot and fidgeted with the zipper.

When he stepped closer to her, she backed up against the wall, clutching her boot. She looked down at his blue jeans, and then up toward his gray cotton shirt and the sinewy muscles of his arms. He was fit and cut, like a kickboxer—but not overly bulky.

"What aren't you telling me, Phoebe?"

She looked up at him and swallowed. "What do you mean?"

He placed his hands on either side of her against the wall. She could smell him again, like when he'd held her in bed. This close, she could see the flecks of gold in his brown eyes.

"You're hiding something, Phoebe. I want to know what it is."

Why did he keep using her name? Was that some type of Marine Corps Special Operations intimidation or interrogation technique? She couldn't think with him so close.

"Stop. You're frightening me."

"You're not frightened."

"I'm not?"

"I'm not going to kiss you, Phoebe."

"You're not?" Was that disappointment or relief in her voice? She couldn't tell.

"You haven't earned my trust. I'm not intimate with women I don't trust." He pressed himself closer to her.

She looked at his lips and then back into his face. "You won't trust me, even if I tell you the truth." By the time she'd finished spilling the news that she'd been conversing with a ghost this whole time, Oz would be on the first plane back to the States.

His level gaze remained unrelenting. "Phoebe?"

She deflated and looked at the ground. "The reason I know you worked for a Special Operations branch of the Marines is because Amyrtaeus told me."

"Amyrtaeus?" Oz leaned back from her. "The dead pharaoh?"

"Yes. I can see his ghost."

Oz retreated a step, his lips curled in a slight smile. "Well, I didn't see *that* coming. I thought you were going to tell me you had bad debt, or had committed a white-collar crime or something."

She shook her head, hugging her boot to her chest. "No."

"How long have you been seeing ghosts?" He crossed his arms.

"Just 'ghost.' Singular. My sister, though, she's seen them all her life." Phoebe watched Oz.

He looked contemplative rather than skeptical. Surely, any moment, he'd make a move to pack his bags.

"And Amyrtaeus is your 'secret in' on how you'll find this tomb?"

"Yes. He wants to find the tomb his wife was buried in and join her in the afterlife." Afterlife? Phoebe wondered: Is that what was next?

"You're... You're doing this for a relationship?"

Phoebe rolled one shoulder. "If Amyrtaeus moves on, then I don't have to be haunted by him anymore. And a discovery this big would be amazing for my museum."

Oz tilted his head to one side with a look suggesting he doubted her words again. "He's linked to something, right? Aren't ghosts usually linked to a person or object? All you need to do is get rid of the object."

Phoebe remembered Gigi telling her something similar, but it didn't apply to all ghosts. She thought of the emerald she'd traveled with here. "I guess I could have done that, but the thought of refusing to help Amyrtaeus seems cruel. How do *you* know about ghosts?"

Oz sat on the end of the bed. "My team and I were behind enemy lines in Afghanistan, and we were pinned down. One of our team—we actually called him Ghost— led us through ten miles of enemy territory, all while navigating unseen by the insurgents. He always had a sixth sense on missions. He confided in me once that the spirit of a fallen comrade was his guardian angel. This angel had told him where to take our team to remain undetected.

"When a man saves your life and gives the ghost of a soldier the credit, you tend to sit up and pay attention. I did a little research after that."

Phoebe sat down in the lounge chair near the window. "You... you believe me?"

"I believe an otherwise rational woman *thinks* she sees a ghost and feels compelled to help him. I can accept that, and I'm willing to help you. But..."

Phoebe cringed. Was he going to force her to seek medical attention? What was in her future? Electroshock therapy? Lobotomy?

"...that still doesn't explain the fear you're carrying around, or the nightmare you had."

Phoebe shook her head. "Amyrtaeus spooked me is all. No pun intended. He senses some type of danger. He says I'm not the only one after the tomb or hoping to make a new discovery."

"And Amyrtaeus' words of caution are the reason you hired me?"

She shook her head. "I would have done so anyway. I don't want to navigate a foreign country on my own, except for England. I could handle England. But I didn't know TJ was going to recommend a Special Operations, former Marine. This whole thing must seem preposterous to you."

"Amyrtaeus is the one who told you I used to work for special ops?"

"Yes, he compared you to the Medja. They were elite paramilitary in the New Kingdom of Egypt, before fading to work in the shadows after the Twentieth Dynasty."

"Yet despite hiring me and knowing my qualifications, you still don't seem reassured."

"I guess hiring you only added to the fear that you'd leave me if you discovered the truth."

"Well, now I know the truth, and, as you can see, I'm not leaving. I don't leave a job half-done, and I agreed to help you find the tomb."

Job. She was just a job, and Oz finished the jobs he started. She could live with that.

"I feel better. Thank you."

WHILE PHOEBE DRESSED, Oz waited in the hotel lobby and called TJ.

"Ozzy, what news?"

"I wanted to give you an update. We're in Cairo. We'll be headed to the tomb site within two hours."

"You two work fast. How's my sister? I don't think she's traveled this much in her entire life."

Oz thought about the nightmare. "Tired, I think. She's a little skittish, too."

"Skittish?"

"Yeah. Has she ever been in any kind of trouble or danger?"

"Phoebe? I'd be surprised if she was ever a day late paying her electric bill. She even pays her taxes on time. She's a straight arrow. How much trouble or danger can a museum curator get into? She works with artifacts and ancient relics all day. Why do you ask?"

Oz paced the marble floor. "Just a feeling. Probably nothing." If she wanted to tell her brother about seeing ghosts, that was her place, not Oz's.

"I remember your intuition being frighteningly accurate, so if you sense something, watch your back. Watch my sister's back first, then yours."

Watch Phoebe's back. Oz had been doing more than that. He'd held her in his arms. He'd pinned her against a wall and fantasized about kissing her.

She entered the lobby and walked toward him with long, confident strides. The museum curator on a mission had replaced the woman afraid of her dreams. She wore dark brown boots, tan pants, a blue cotton blouse, and a vest. Her hair was pulled back into a bun. A backpack was slung over one shoulder.

"I've got her back," Oz told TJ. "I'll call you when we're done here." Oz turned off his phone and slipped it into his pocket.

Phoebe smiled as she approached, and Oz's mind instantly snapped to visions of her in his arms. He wanted to kiss each of her dimples before burying his face in her neck.

Instead, he cleared his throat. "Are you going to a dig site? Or English horseback riding?"

"I'll have you know these boots are high enough that I won't have a speck of sand get between my toes, and the shirt is light and airy, perfect for hot weather."

"You look very nice. Breakfast?"

"Just coffee and I'll be set."

"You're in for a treat. They make Turkish coffee at a cafe down the street. Thick and delicious—and no sippy cups."

∽

KENNETH WATCHED PHOEBE FROM A DISTANCE. The museum curator sat at a cafe drinking Turkish coffee with a man—the same man she'd driven to D.C. to see, before that man had joined her for this trip to Egypt. He wasn't one of Phoebe's many brothers, so he must be a friend or long-distance lover.

Kenneth could see Amyrtaeus standing near their table, listening and occasionally being included in the conversation. Did Phoebe's boyfriend see ghosts? Kenneth couldn't tell. The man didn't appear to make eye contact with Amyrtaeus.

The pharaoh needed to lead Phoebe to the untouched tomb, still filled with treasure, so Kenneth could claim it as his own. The gravesite, undiscovered since being sealed, would contain the riches of the ancient Egyptian elite buried there.

Phoebe's boyfriend, assuming that's what he was, added an unknown element to the equation. He was svelte and observant, always scanning his surroundings. This was not a man on a leisurely vacation with a beautiful woman. Judging from the way the man watched Phoebe, and watched out for her, there was intimacy between them.

The man's presence was inconvenient.

Kenneth had counted on Phoebe bringing her sister, a

powerful medium, to Egypt. They'd be two women without connections in a foreign country. Instead, Phoebe had brought her boyfriend. Well, Kenneth could work around the mishap. Regardless of this man's size, stealth, or keen eyes, he wasn't bulletproof.

CHAPTER 6

*O*z ordered coffee for them at Cafe Corniche, just a few blocks from their hotel. They sat at a small table outdoors.

"Did you schedule any leisure time into this trip?" he asked. "It might be nice to play tourist and see some sights."

"The return trip is in five days, so while sightseeing would be nice, time may be too tight." Phoebe's words came out hesitantly.

He suspected the source of her hesitation was the fact that he was employed by her. Extra days of protection would cost more. "Vacation days won't count toward my bill," he reassured her.

Phoebe frowned. "That's not fair to you." She sipped her Turkish coffee. "Wow. This is delicious."

"If I'm getting to sightsee in my family's country of origin, it's more than fair." He drank his coffee. "Now, tell me about Amyrtaeus."

Phoebe seemed a bit more comfortable with this topic of conversation. "Well, he isn't a well-known pharaoh." Phoebe glanced to her right. "Sorry, but it's true." She faced Oz again. "His rule was from 404 B.C. To 399 B.C, and he was the only pharaoh from the twenty-eighth Dynasty. However, he ended the Persian occupation of Egypt—at least of the Delta—through a revolt he led against Persian King Darius II. That independence lasted for sixty years. That's no minor accomplishment."

"But he only ruled for five years."

"*Nearly* six," she corrected him.

Oz suspected the correction had actually come from Amyrtaeus.

"His army was defeated by Nepherites I of Mendes, and Amyrtaeus was executed in Memphis in 399 B.C. There are no monuments to him—and because he was defeated in battle, he was buried in an unmarked grave."

"So Nepherites was the twenty-ninth dynasty."

"Yes, he only ruled for six years before his own death and was then succeeded by his son."

"And Amyrtaeus' wife?"

"There aren't any records of her—but Amyrtaeus tells me that Chione fled and lived in hiding for two years. She later remarried to a wealthy Egyptian who had a high enough ranking to earn her a ritual burial in a tomb with others of similar status. She kept scrolls that documented Amyrtaeus' rule, and Amyrtaeus believes they're still buried with her. He also wants to make sure she's moved on and isn't lingering in this world, waiting for him before she crosses to the next."

"If Amyrtaeus is connected to the emerald, what's his wife connected to?"

Phoebe cocked her head to one side, listening. "A ruby. They were wedding gifts to each other. The emerald signified fertility and rebirth, and the Egyptians believed that when a ruby touched a woman's skin, it would grant her prosperity and love."

Oz drank the last of his coffee. His thoughts swam in a sea of intrigue. He'd never imagined ancient history could be so riveting. He'd studied modern history ad nauseam, because it helped him understand cultures, and understanding cultures helped him in the many countries he traveled to.

Sitting outside at a café, with a view of the Nile River behind them, Oz wondered how he'd ever survive at a desk job doing cryptography. He thought he'd wanted to be more stationary after years of travel, but six months of being stationary back in the US had made him restless. Traveling freely like this—no covert missions, no back-alley meetings—appealed to him. Was there a job in which he could travel as protection for international clients?

He glanced at Phoebe. Oz suspected part of the enjoyment of his current role was this beautiful, charming museum curator. Employment like this wouldn't be the same if he was working for someone else.

Phoebe glanced at her watch. "We've an hour to spare before our scheduled ride to the Hawara pyramid. Do you want to go for a walk?"

. . .

PHOEBE WALKED beside Oz along the great Nile River. The morning sun glistened on the surface.

"The longest river in the world," she marveled.

"Over four-thousand miles." Oz stuck his hands in his pockets. "I like walking along the river in every city I've traveled to."

"Hmm. And what rivers have you walked along?"

"Other parts of the Nile. The Tigris, the Bogota, the Pearl, the Danube, the Thames, the Moskva, the Seine, the Moldau."

Phoebe associated the countries as he talked: Iraq, Colombia, China, Hungary, England, Russia, France, and the Czech Republic. "Amyrtaeus implied the work you did was dangerous." She rushed to add: "He didn't mention any specifics."

"Yes, it was dangerous."

"You're retired now. Seems early for retirement."

"I served my country for ten years. Long enough to do some good. Long enough to get shot."

"Was it bad? Or, I mean, you don't have to tell me that."

He arched an eyebrow. "Took a bullet to my right shoulder. I didn't lose any function, but I do have chronic pain. I wasn't fit for service after that. Now that physical therapy is over, I'll start my next job."

"And cybersecurity is next?"

"Yeah. The work will be interesting and potentially still offer the opportunity for travel."

"If you're ever in Hershey, I've got a nice little museum you can drop by and see." Phoebe linked her arm through his.

When he took a moment to reply, she instantly felt

foolish for the flirtation. Of course, he wouldn't want to see her museum…

She started to pull her arm back.

"I'd love to see it." He pinned her arm between his elbow and ribs.

Phoebe relaxed, and they walked with their arms linked. With her free hand, she tucked a strand of hair behind her ear.

"When do we get to see Hamunaptra?"

She puzzled for a moment before she saw the playful twinkle in Oz's eyes. With a nudge of her elbow into his arm, she said, "*That* is a fictional city created solely for *The Mummy* movie. Now, Cairo does have a City of the Dead. It's four miles of dense tombs and mausoleum structures."

"So, we won't be discovering the *Book of the Dead* and raising any mummies?"

"Many *Book of the Dead* have been discovered. They were often found in tombs. Now that I've seen the ghost of an Egyptian pharaoh, I can't say definitively that ancient scrolls couldn't raise a mummy—or at least the ghost of a mummy. But we're here to set one free, not collect any more."

"Set *two* free."

"Right, two."

Oz squeezed her arm with his, and she smiled.

"So, Ozymandias. Amyrtaeus tells me your name means 'King of Kings'. It was Rameses II's name."

"Yes, well, in Shelley's poem it's King of Kings. In strict Greek translation it's: *King of Air*, which, according to your brother, means King of Nothing."

"Oh, nonsense. Leave it to TJ to turn something

magnificent into something humbling. I think King of Air is appropriate for a soldier. A warrior. King of Air. It even sounds stealthy. I wouldn't want to face the King of Air in a dark alley or treacherous jungle."

"You wouldn't?" He winked at her.

"Well, unless it was specifically *you*. You, I'd meet anywhere."

When he smiled as he looked into her eyes, an attraction sizzled through her in the weight of his gaze. Warmth tingled through her and had her remembering how close he'd been to her in their hotel room.

'I'm not going to kiss you, Phoebe.'

'You're not?'

Right. The man did not want to kiss her.

She cleared her throat. "Ready to walk back?" Her voice sounded a little dry and husky. "It's a two-hour drive to the Hawara pyramid and the dig site is just outside of that."

Oz nodded. "Ready."

PHOEBE KEPT the lanyard visible around her neck as she led Oz through the dig site. The mid-morning sun rose in the distance, and the day was growing warm. Excavators with hand-held tools worked in deep pits, gouged far into the ground, many parting around the openings of the chambers beneath the sand. This current dig had uncovered a few rooms and one tomb. Dust and sand that had been stirred up swirled along the surface of the ground, almost as if it had a life of its own.

In the backdrop, rose the rounded, eroded mound of the Hawara pyramid. This pyramid of the twelfth dynasty had been excavated and explored from the mid to late 1800s. They'd discovered one-hundred-and-forty-six coffins there, exquisitely decorated with portraits painted on them.

Oz walked beside Phoebe, silently observing the surroundings. He'd chosen khaki pants, a white button shirt, and worn work-boots for the excursion. Phoebe still marveled that he'd taken the unveiling of her secret about the ghostly pharaoh in his stride. He seemed to be starting to trust her.

As they walked deeper into the dig site, she spotted a college-aged student wearing a UAB T-shirt. She asked the student to direct them to Tremaine Johnson, the project manager. The woman pointed her and Oz in his direction, and Phoebe found Tremaine at the southwest corner of the site, teaching a group of students.

Phoebe waved, and the project manager gave her a puzzled look before stepping away from the group to meet her.

She extended a hand. "Phoebe Montgomery."

Tremaine shook it, sand and grit on his dark-skinned palm. He looked at her lanyard. "Oh—Sara's friend! Yes, she said you were coming. I guess I didn't realize it would be so soon."

"Thanks for letting me tour the place. I've got the 'Pharaohs and Phantoms' Egyptian Exhibit on loan in my museum and with it, the urge to see a real-life dig. This is my friend, Oz Levine." She was speaking too fast, and she hoped it would be perceived as excitement at having the opportunity to observe the excavation rather than her intention to explore the unexplored.

Tremaine shook Oz's hand.

The project manager took off his fedora, revealing a bald head. "Well, as you can see, it's mostly sand." He swiped a handkerchief over his head, pocketed it, and put his hat back on. "You're welcome to explore. I'll tell you the same thing I tell my students: Watch where you step, and nothing is 'finder's keepers'."

"Understood."

Tremaine pointed across the dig site. "Two of the openings are just dead-end rooms. The other is a larger burial chamber. You can't go in there without an escort. If you want to go in, ask one of my team and they'll accompany you."

"Okay."

Amyrtaeus dissolved into view. "We don't want that one anyway. I know a faster route." His gaze roamed the landscape. "Nothing looks remotely familiar," he complained.

"It's twenty-five-hundred years old," Phoebe reminded the ghost.

"That's right," Tremaine agreed. "Treat it as such."

"Absolutely." Phoebe nodded.

She thanked Tremaine again and left to start her exploration. As she followed Amyrtaeus, Oz followed her. Together, they took a ladder down to the excavated maze and followed the path around to the entryway, which the dig director had declared was a dead end.

Inside the dim room, Phoebe pulled out her flashlight and swung it around the walls. The worn brick was devoid of markings. She suspected the entry room was too close to the surface to have survived with preserved drawings.

Oz inspected the room with his flashlight as well. "I can see why Tremaine called this a dead end."

"Oh, have faith," Amyrtaeus said. "Miss Montgomery, if you would be so kind as to stand in the northeast corner. Now, have Mr. Levine stand in the opposite corner. There, you'll activate the pressure-sensitive plates."

Phoebe hesitantly walked to one corner, as she recalled her nightmare—black sarcophagus, falling sand, and darkness.

It had only been a dream. Right?

When Phoebe took her position, she turned around to face Oz. "Can you stand in the opposite corner from me?"

Oz walked toward the corner. "Now what?"

"A secret entrance, I think."

Oz stood in the corner and turned to face Phoebe. Nothing happened.

Amyrtaeus stroked his fake beard. "Perhaps they've crusted over time."

"Centuries of alternating seasons, temperatures, and humidity could have made them hard to move," Phoebe agreed. "They might need more weight."

She jumped up and down in her corner. "Try jumping."

Oz arched an eyebrow. "I'm *not* jumping."

"Please?" She hopped again.

Oz tried jumping, but again nothing happened.

"Together on the count of three," Phoebe said.

She counted, and they jumped together. Two triangular slabs in the floor suddenly moved. They lowered, tips down, spilling sand into the darkness below. Phoebe and Oz lost their footing on the steep incline and slid down toward each other, toward the pit suddenly forming in the center of the room.

CHAPTER 7

*a*s they fell toward the black hole, Oz grabbed Phoebe roughly around the waist, pulled her close, and wrapped his body around her.

The fall was short, but they lost their balance when their feet struck the sand. Oz spun to take the fall, and she landed on top of him.

Oz let out a grunt.

"I'm so sorry! Are you okay?" She stood and dusted the sand off her pants. She appreciated how his fast reflexes had spared her serious bruising.

"I don't suppose Amyrtaeus mentioned a ten-foot plummet?"

"No."

"I bet you've got sand in your boots *now*." Oz grinned, pushing himself to his feet.

She gave him a scowl, which only served to widen his grin.

The ceiling plates, which had swung open and dropped them into this tomb, began to close. Oz leaped into the air, clinging to the triangular corner of one of them. It pulled him off his feet as he clung to it, biceps straining. "How do we keep it from sealing us in?"

"I don't know."

"You can't," Amyrtaeus said.

With the ceiling almost shut, Oz was forced to let go. He landed back on his feet with cat-like agility.

"There will be other ways out," the pharaoh promised.

"Amyrtaeus says we'll find another way out."

Oz snatched up his flashlight. "Will we? Because there are so many entrances and exits that this place hasn't been discovered in nearly three-thousand years."

Phoebe could feel his irritation rippling through the sarcasm in his voice like sunrays off hot concrete. She couldn't blame him. She didn't want to be entombed alive in an ancient burial room either.

The ceiling sealed shut, leaving their flashlights as the only source of light.

"I'm sorry," Phoebe said.

"Stop apologizing. Let's just get through this."

She pulled two masks out of her backpack and handed one to Oz.

He gave her a quizzical look.

"HEPA-filtered mask," she explained. "You don't want to breathe whatever's been lurking, unventilated, down here for millennia."

He frowned.

"You want sexy? Or you want a mask?" She wriggled it in the air.

"Are those my only options?"

Her cheeks burned red. "I meant: Do you want to *look*

sexy—and contract a lung disease—or hide that handsome face behind a mask and stay healthy?"

"I liked your first question better." He grinned.

After tossing a mask at him, she pulled hers on. She began to explore the chamber they were inside. It was square-shaped, with three solid walls and the fourth bearing an archway leading to a hallway beyond.

Phoebe examined the painted drawings on the wall. Numerous hieroglyphs surrounded a painting of Ra, the sun god. His hawk-head was crowned with a solar disk, and he wore a white skirt over his red skin. White-robed Egyptians knelt at his feet, arms raised in worship into the air.

"They ground minerals to make red, black, blue, yellow, and white paint. Charcoal for black. Calcium compounds for white. Azurite for blue. Iron oxide for red and yellow. The mineral dust was added to plant glue and then painted on the walls over a thin layer of plaster. It's quite intricate."

"It's exquisite," Oz said.

Phoebe took her phone out and snapped pictures of the drawing—rivers with fish swimming, crops growing under a vibrant sun, Egyptians working and worshiping. Turning toward the hallway, she took pictures of the decorative archway.

"CAN YOU TELL WHAT IT SAYS?" Oz asked.

He walked around, performing his own inspection of the room. He was amazed by the intricate detail of the wall paintings. He was also amazed at Phoebe's enthusiasm. She was like a kid in a candy store.

She focused on the hieroglyphics and struggled through the translation. "Mother of heaven... Hail to thee... Offerings of ox and antelope... Bathe in power and glory." She skimmed through it. "It reads like a prayer."

"No mummy's curse?"

"No curses."

She took another photo. "I'm sorry. I know you want to get out of here."

"Relax. We're here. Enjoy it and take your photos. This is a once in a lifetime opportunity. No one has seen this in thousands of years."

"Thank you." She walked over to him. "And thank you for coming." Phoebe wrapped her arms, flashlight in one hand and phone in he other, around him. "I couldn't have done this without you."

He was startled at first but then quickly returned the hug. "You're welcome."

Leaning back, she smiled at him. He stared back, deep into the liquid green of her eyes. He wasn't dreaming the chemistry between them, right? If not for the masks, he might have kissed her then.

"Ready to find out what's behind archway number one?"

"Ready," Oz said, though didn't like that the embrace ended so soon.

When Phoebe pocketed her phone, Oz took her free hand and positioned her slightly behind him. "But I go first."

She let him lead. "You're taking this protection detail extremely seriously."

He glanced back at her. "I hope by now you know it's more than that."

Even in the peripheral glow of her flashlight, he could tell she blushed.

Cautiously, Oz proceeded forward, aware of every sound and shift of sand and dirt beneath his feet. He was reminded of the Colombian jungle he'd once navigated during a dangerous hostage extraction. Every step had grown more treacherous as he and his team had approached the drug cartel camp. His team was in enemy territory—foreign to him, but well-known to their armed enemies. He had to be cognizant of tripwires, booby traps, and jungle spies who could open fire at any moment.

Oz brought his mind back to the tomb where, so far, nothing seemed dangerous. When he and Phoebe had been topside, not long after having met Tremaine, Oz had felt the weird sensation of being watched. Yet, when he'd scanned the excavation site, he'd seen nothing suspicious.

But Amyrtaeus had warned Phoebe of danger. *He says I'm not the only one after making a new discovery.*

Inside the tomb, breathing the dry, cool air through their masks, Oz and Phoebe slowly descended a series of steps they'd come across.

Were they being followed? How would anyone suspect a museum curator would be helpful in finding an undiscovered section of a tomb? Except Phoebe wasn't the only person who could see ghosts. Oz had experienced first-hand the power of a medium when his comrade on the battlefield had claimed to see an apparition, who he'd credited for his uncanny ability to navigate enemy territory and get their team to safety. Not to mention, Oz believed Phoebe's description of her sister's ability.

Was someone tracking Amyrtaeus? Somebody who could see him the same way Phoebe could?

They finally approached a large rectangular room.

PHOEBE'S EXCITEMENT swelled as she and Oz walked deeper into the tomb. No one had walked across these flagstones in over two thousand years. When they passed through a hallway toward another chamber, she paused to read the archway hieroglyphics.

"The dead shall rest."

"That would seem to suggest we're close to the corpses," Oz said.

"Chione is in that chamber," Amyrtaeus said, his voice breathless with anticipation.

Phoebe glanced at Oz, who seemed on edge. "Relax. This is the fun part."

"You're not worried about booby traps?"

She adjusted her mask. "Egyptian tombs don't have elaborate traps like in an Indiana Jones movie."

"No?"

"Secret chambers? Yes. Darts flying out of walls? No."

Phoebe and Oz walked into the chamber, their flashlights held high as they inspected the room. Three feet in from each wall were columns standing about four-feet-tall, made from clay. Recessed into the walls were dozens of graves, all with bone remnants that had been buried there over two-thousand years ago.

"Which one is your wife?"

"On the left. Third from the bottom," Amyrtaeus answered.

Phoebe looked back at the entranceway. "Why aren't you coming in?"

Amyrtaeus frowned. "I can't. The inscriptions on the arch prevent spirits from crossing—out *or* in. They're the reason Chione's spirit has never left this room."

"Okay. I'll bring her to you."

Phoebe set her flashlight on one of the columns and extended the outer sheath. The flashlight transformed into a lantern, casting a wide white glow.

"Aren't *you* the well-equipped explorer?" Oz mused.

"I was a Girl Scout." She winked at him and took his flashlight from him.

She approached the grave recess and carefully inspected the remains in the bright beam of the flashlight. "There aren't any canopic jars." But she did see a dust-covered stone and reached for it.

Oz rested a hand on Phoebe's forearm, stopping her mid-reach. "Phoebe." He pulled the mask down from his face. "What if she's not here? What if her spirit has already moved on?"

She pulled her mask down and looked into Oz's eyes. Concern. Compassion. Her heart melted to think he'd emotionally invested in this endeavor.

"Amyrtaeus would be okay with that. If she's moved on, then he'll know she had happiness. He just didn't want to take the chance she waited here for him."

"That's a long time to wait."

The warmth of Oz's touch radiated through Phoebe's

arm. His proximity in the darkened room caused her heartbeat to accelerate.

She licked her lips. "What's a few thousand years in an eternity? Maybe Chione had no better place to be. Maybe Amyrtaeus was worth waiting for."

The peripheral glow of the flashlight accentuated Oz's smile. By the entrance, Amyrtaeus cleared his throat.

Phoebe straightened. "Right. Stone." She reached for it, retrieved it, and cleaned off the thick coat of dust.

Oz took the flashlight and set it up like a lantern on one of the columns, just as Phoebe had done with the other.

The red sheen of the stone she held began to glow. A translucent woman suddenly appeared, with rich, dark skin and long, silky brown hair.

This must be Chione, Phoebe thought.

The woman wore an ankle-length, cream-colored linen dress adorned with gold-painted beads. Her sculptured oval face bore strong cheekbones and thick eyelashes.

She started speaking in a rushed and heated tone to Phoebe.

"What's happening?" Oz asked.

"She's here. She's talking, but I've no idea what she's saying. She's probably cursing us for defiling sacred burial grounds."

Amyrtaeus had hundreds of years outside of his tomb to learn English (and perhaps other languages), and his trapped wife only spoke ancient Egyptian.

Phoebe swung her arms toward the archway where Amyrtaeus stood. The Egyptian woman's eyes followed the path of Phoebe's gesture, and then Chione gasped. She talked with excited animation, in a stream of dialogue from which Phoebe only understood the intermittent word 'Amyrtaeus.' Chione walked right up to the spiritual threshold as Phoebe followed behind her with the glowing ruby.

When Phoebe reached the archway, Amyrtaeus' eyes brimmed with tears. His wife strained to escape the room to reach him. Phoebe crossed the threshold with the ruby, and his wife followed.

The ghostly couple wept with joy as they embraced. Phoebe stepped back and watched, feeling her own eyes grow moist. With the two spirits intertwined, Phoebe couldn't tell where one began and the other ended.

"They're together," she whispered to Oz.

With one arm around his wife's waist, Amyrtaeus turned toward Phoebe. "Many blessings on you, your family, and Mr. Levine. What you did for me will never be forgotten. The spirits will watch over you and protect you all your life, and you will enjoy other adventures." He started to fade.

"Wait, wait, wait! We need to know how to get out of here," Phoebe demanded.

"The spirits of the dead will guide you."

With that, Amyrtaeus and Chione faded into a sparkling swarm of gold dust, before vanishing entirely.

Phoebe started to open her mouth in protest, but the pharaoh was already gone.

What?

'Spirits will guide you?'

Phoebe didn't want any more spirits! One had been stressful enough.

She turned to Oz. "It was beautiful. They're together, and they moved on."

"Well done."

"Well done indeed." A deep male voice suddenly sounded behind Phoebe.

She jumped, recoiling back into the chamber with Oz who caught her arms and pulled her protectively behind him.

Looking around Oz, she saw a man pointing a gun at them.

CHAPTER 8

"*K*enny?"

Phoebe hadn't seen the lying, cheating scoundrel in over eight years, but she instantly recognized the slanting blue eyes and easy, self-assured posture of her former lover.

Professor Kenneth Richards' hair was salt and pepper now, instead of brown, but it only made him look more distinguished.

Confusion and fear riveted Phoebe to where she stood. "What are you doing here?" A terrible sense of dread told her she really didn't want to know.

"Isn't it obvious? I'm here for the treasure." Kenny extended a hand to sweep the room.

Phoebe looked down at the ruby she held. "But how did you know to follow me?"

"I set up this entire expedition! Well, except for *him*." Kenny jutted his chin toward Oz.

"I don't understand," Phoebe said.

"Of course you don't." Kenny's condescending tone

sent a wave of anger through Phoebe—one that had her temples throbbing.

Through clenched teeth, she asked, "Why don't you explain it to me, *Professor Richards?*"

Kenny kept his gun on Oz as he spoke. "The ability of a medium can run in families. You confided in me—I believe after just two glasses of wine and some *delightful* intimacy—that your sister could converse with spirits. Now, what's her name again?"

Phoebe pursed her lips shut. She tried to move from around Oz, but he kept his body in front of her.

"Anyway," Kenneth continued, "you also confided once that you heard things, too—whispers sometimes, around certain pieces of artwork. I'd always suspected that perhaps the same ability was in you, just not fully manifested. I advocated for the Egyptian exhibit to be sent to your museum. I even wrote letters on your behalf for your tiny, insignificant museum. You're welcome, by the way."

"You wanted Amyrtaeus to reveal himself to me?" Phoebe's hands rested on Oz's biceps, which were rock hard with coiled tension. She wondered what ticked off the retired Marine more—being held at gunpoint or Kenny's scheming.

"I'd hoped he'd speak to you—*confide* in you." Kenny kept the entrance to the tomb blocked as he took another step into the chamber. "The arrogant pharaoh wouldn't tell me how to find this place. I thought you'd bring your sister on the treasure hunt, though, since she's the real talent between the two of you. I guess you brought your boyfriend instead."

"This wasn't a treasure hunt!" Phoebe snapped. "Amyrtaeus wanted to be reunited with his wife!"

Kenny rolled his eyes. "Yes, the high and mighty pharaoh nobody knows or cares about gave me the same sob story. Then, he clammed up—and refused to tell me where to find his beloved wife."

"You're the dangerous one he warned me about." Phoebe had no idea that Kenny could also see spirits. Then again, he hadn't even bothered to mention he was married while they'd been dating.

"He's dead. What use does he have for ancient artifacts and gemstones? None. Amyrtaeus was just being selfish."

"Why did you think he'd confide in me?"

Kenny answered with a smirk. Phoebe understood as soon as she saw the expression. Kenny had known that Amyrtaeus would see she was compassionate. She was a bleeding heart, like the young college student who'd had an affair with her professor. Maybe Phoebe truly had learned nothing.

Her hand found its way into Oz's.

No, not nothing. She'd learned, if nothing else, that there *were* good and honest men in this world. Men like Amyrtaeus and men like Oz. Phoebe's emotions had led her to help one and develop feelings for another.

She placed the ruby on one of the columns nearest to her and Oz. Kenny could have the treasure he sought if he really wanted it so badly. Phoebe had Oz *and* a clean conscience, knowing her moral compass pointed north.

"Good girl. Now, go from grave to grave and pull out more. Your silent, glowering boyfriend can help you."

"You're not going to kill us?" Oz asked.

"Not if you collect more. This doesn't have to get ugly."

Phoebe began the search, squinting and straining to look into the graves. *Things are already ugly*, she thought. Kenny wasn't going to rob the graves and leave witnesses.

Son of scarab! Phoebe swore to herself.

How would he do it? How would he kill them?

Surely not the gun. Bullets would be traceable and lead to an investigation. He could try to collapse the archway and trap them down here. They might never be found if Kenny took the riches and left the chamber closed. She and Oz would die of suffocation. But the underground Egyptian tombs were known to have shafts. If they found one and opened it, they *might* have a chance at escape.

Pulling a gold necklace from among the bones, she silently apologized to the person it once belonged to. She set it on the column alongside the ruby. Oz followed suit with a string of dusty pearls.

Phoebe glanced at him, wishing she could apologize for unknowingly dragging him into a trap. He'd probably tell her to stop apologizing. She smiled at that...

...before her temper flared again.

Darn Kenny, and his elaborate trap!

It would have been easy for Kenny to track her, since she'd made no secret about the trip. Anyone at the museum could have told him when Phoebe had left for Egypt. She'd registered at the hotel in Cairo under her own name. All he needed to do was follow her—with a gun. If it weren't for the weapon, she was certain Oz would have clobbered Kenny by now.

A voice, emerging from the bones of the nearest

corpse, suddenly caught Phoebe's attention. She listened intently.

Gibberish.

She didn't speak ancient Egyptian. "I don't understand," she whispered.

"What?" Kenny snapped.

"I don't understand why you're doing this."

Oz placed two sapphire earrings on the column. His movements were slow and deliberate, as if waiting for an opening to attack Kenny.

"Money," Kenny retorted.

When Phoebe turned back to the next set of bones to search them, gold-glowing hieroglyphics shone on the back wall of the grave—where only she could see.

When the lights dim, pull the sconce.

Lights dim? And who was sending her this message?

She glanced around the chamber and saw the sconce on the wall opposite the archway, right where Kenny stood with his gun in hand. *Pull the sconce.* She tried to memorize its exact height on the wall so she could find it in the dark.

But how to warn Oz? He wouldn't see the spirit—and he'd be in the dark if the spirit disrupted the light from the lanterns.

As Oz passed her toward the next grave, Phoebe made brief eye contact and pulled the mask from around her neck and back up over her mouth and nose. Oz mimicked

her. He might not know what was going to happen—
neither did she—but he now knew to be prepared.

Rumbling sounded from the center of the room.
Phoebe turned to look at the column where they'd laid the
plundered riches. Spirits—some just wisps of color and
others entire translucent bodies—suddenly spewed forth.

"What's happening?" Kenny demanded. He pointed his
gun at the varying spirits, but didn't fire.

"I think we've upset the spirits of the dead by
disturbing their graves."

"Phoebe?" Oz came to stand by her side.

Oz couldn't see what was happening, even as ghosts
swirled around the chamber. To him, it would appear as
though only the flashlights were flickering.

Kenny's hands shook. "Make them stop." He took steps
backward as they circled the ceiling until he backed into
the wall.

"I don't know how to make them stop," she said.

While that was true, Kenny only needed to step on the
other side of the archway to escape them. Phoebe doubted
Kenny knew hieroglyphics or had bothered to read the
inscription over the archway even if he did.

The swarm of spirits, murmuring and chanting,
coalesced like a giant black cloud on the ceiling before
falling into the room. Phoebe snatched a flashlight as she
ducked toward the ground. The light extinguished, and all
three of them were plunged into blackness.

Kenny screamed. He fired once, twice. She heard
grunts and the sound of fists connecting with flesh.
Reaching the wall, she felt for the sconce. Her fingertips

touched cold, rusty metal. She pulled with all her might and moved the sconce like a lever, yanking it downward.

"Oz!" Could he find her in the dark?

The spirits shifted back from her like the parting of the Red Sea, and Phoebe's flashlight suddenly shimmered back to life. In the light, Oz ran to her.

Beside her, a brick wall had swung open, revealing a hidden room. As the two of them scurried inside, the door closed shut behind them.

Oz HELD Phoebe's hand in one of his, and the gun he'd snatched from Kenneth in the other. When the door behind them closed, he exhaled a tentative sigh of relief. They stood in yet another chamber. His heart started to slow after the fight with Kenny.

Phoebe dropped the flashlight and ran her hands over Oz's arms and torso. "Are you okay? Are you shot?" She tugged off her mask.

"I'm okay."

She clung to him in a hug. "Oh, thank God. I'm sorry. I'm *so* sorry. I had no idea Kenny set this all up—that he'd manipulated me."

Oz slipped the gun into his belt. With one arm wrapped around Phoebe, he pulled his mask off with the other. "It's okay. I know. I realize that."

She stepped back. "Sorry."

"Stop apologizing."

Oz pulled her roughly against him, pressing her body against his. His eyes roamed her face down to Phoebe's sweet, succulent lips. "I'm going to kiss you now."

"You are?"

"I'm not going to apologize for it."

"Does that mean you trust me?"

"I do."

Before he could close the gap to kiss Phoebe, she moved in and pressed her mouth against his. As the kiss deepened, she parted her lips. His tongue explored the soft warmth of her mouth. Her rumbling moan of pleasure had him drenched in arousal.

When Oz finally pulled away, they were both breathless.

Phoebe's cheeks were a perfect pink. "That was amazing."

"I thought so, too."

"But we probably shouldn't do things that make us consume excess oxygen. Not until we're out of here. I'm not sure what the oxygen supply is like in a sealed room sixty feet below the surface."

"Fair point," he said. "We'll save our oxygen-consuming activities for later." Oz felt lightheaded. He was certain that was from the impact Phoebe had on him, though, and not the oxygen levels. He nipped at her bottom lip before releasing her.

Their current room was considerably smaller than the chamber full of graves. Oz suspected Kenneth had days of oxygen, with his room connected to the passageways and other chambers.

Oz picked up the flashlight and swung it around the small, square room they now stood inside. On the floor beneath them was a large, round clay disk. He saw no other doorway, no way out except the way they'd come in.

He didn't see a lever on this side either, so they would need to find another way to open the door.

"Did we just exchange one tomb for another?" he asked.

Phoebe tucked strands of blond hair back behind her ears. "At least this one doesn't have a maniac with a gun in it."

"Any spirits here to show us the way out?"

"We're alone."

"Do any of these hieroglyphics say 'This way out'?"

Phoebe took the flashlight from him and inspected the walls. "'To rise heavenward, see more than what is written.'"

"More? What else is written?" Oz asked.

"I ... I don't know. The other letters don't make words."

"*See more than what is written.*" Oz ran a hand along the hieroglyphics. The same linear column of five symbols was in the center of all four walls. In the middle of the room was another pedestal, like the four in the last room. This one was made of a yellow-ivory limestone.

He set the flashlight on it, extending it back into lantern mode. He stroked the ridges along the column, knocking off dust and sand. Not just ridges. They were more like discs. Each disc had an array of hieroglyphics in the same white, red, and blue paint.

Using his fingers, Oz turned the top disc. The dry sound of limestone grating limestone reverberated in his ears.

But how did they align? The symbols on the walls were the same as those on the discs. If he began where they'd entered, the first symbol was a stork. He lined up the stork on the disc with the stork on the wall. Moving to the next disc, he lined up the eye with the second symbol on the wall. He worked his way clockwise until all the pictures on the discs were lined up in the same order as the pictures on the wall.

Oz stepped back to make sure he was out of the way—but nothing happened.

"It was a good idea," Phoebe offered.

Oz rubbed his neck. "I was hoping the door would open back up, or another door. But maybe it's not the right alignment." He started to turn the first disc again. "We'll just try a different alignment."

When he finished rotating each disc ninety degrees, the floor rumbled.

Phoebe sucked in a breath. "Is this a good thing?"

He reached down and took her hand. "If we trust what you said about no booby traps, then this is a good thing."

The brick plate on which they stood began to rise upward. As it moved, the ceiling slid aside, revealing a shaft above them. High above them, another set of horizontal doors moved. Sand from above poured on either side of Phoebe and Oz as the doors opened.

Oz blinked against the onslaught of bright sunlight. When his eyes adjusted, he could see the dig site in the distance. He pulled Phoebe off the plate with him just as the doors began to close automatically.

She pressed herself closer to him and wrapped her arms around his neck. He wrenched his mask off before tilting his head down to look at her.

"You got us out," Phoebe said. "*Cryptologist.*"

Oz eased his arms around her waist. He looked from

her lips to her eyes, and then back down to her lips again. He wanted to taste her and feel the warmth and softness of her mouth—again, and again.

He leaned closer.

"How'd you end up over here?" Tremaine demanded as he approached.

Phoebe stepped back and turned toward the dig director. "We discovered another chamber. I'll show you!"

CHAPTER 9

*O*z's gaze scrutinized his bleak apartment. He'd been back from Egypt for five days now. He already missed Phoebe, and he missed the adventure they'd shared. Looking down at the email on his laptop, he reread the acceptance email for the cybersecurity position.

A desk job. How long would he last at a desk job?

He and Phoebe had been in different seats on the trip back from Egypt, and so they'd only had a few hours of layover to sit beside each other in silence. What could he say to her?

Do you want to start a long-distance relationship with me?

She had a career and a museum to run. He had a lonely past of secret missions and a future of indecision. Money wasn't a problem. He'd saved and invested most of his earnings from his days in the Marines, because food, lodging, and travel were all paid for by Uncle Sam. But he couldn't date a woman while he was unemployed.

Yet, if he took the cybersecurity position, they would

remain three hours away from each other. Maybe that *was* doable. They could still see each other on weekends. But first, Oz needed to find out if Phoebe wanted to see him again at all, now that the contract-for-hire was over.

At least she was safe. Kenneth had been babbling incoherently when they'd found him in the tomb he'd ransacked. Tremaine instantly swore he'd begin disciplinary proceedings to have Kenneth terminated from his university for defiling an ancient tomb. The dig director had been livid.

Oz's phone rang. "Montgomery."

Unfortunately, it was the brother Montgomery—TJ, and not Phoebe.

"Ozzy. How are you? Phoebe said Egypt went well."

Oz rubbed his neck. "Yeah. Egypt went well. Phoebe found what she was looking for."

"She said the dig director even gave her a little money for the find. Enough to cover trip expenses, anyway."

"She wasn't after money." Neither was Oz. He'd realized that about five minutes into their trip. In fact, he'd told Phoebe not to worry about paying him. She'd transferred the funds anyway, and they'd shown up in his account.

"Huh. What do you think she was after?"

Love, Oz thought. Phoebe wanted to reunite Amyrtaeus with his wife, but in doing so, he realized, she'd also wanted to restore her faith in love in the first place. And her ability to trust in a relationship.

Oz strummed his fingers on his keyboard. "She didn't tell you?"

TJ sighed. "She told me she went to find an undiscovered tomb, but what she ended up finding was a man who made her heart melt."

Oz stood up. "She said *that*?"

"Well, she used the 'L' word, but I can't repeat that. Not when it's my little sister talking about a man."

Oz grinned. "She said she *loves* me?"

TJ groaned. "I can't believe I'm being forced into the role of matchmaker here. I did *not* set you two up, okay? My intentions were to provide her with a security detail. But yes, she likes, maybe even *loves* you. So, I told her that was absurd, because you've only known each other for two weeks. It *is* absurd, right?"

Oz didn't answer. Should he confess to TJ that he shared his sister's feelings?

TJ continued, "Well, I've never heard her so happy, so maybe it's not absurd. Maybe the guy I'd trust on the battlefield is the same guy I'd trust with my sister's heart."

"I kissed her," Oz confessed.

"I did *not* need to know that."

"I *like* her."

"That I do need to know."

"I'd like to date her."

"Well, what are you waiting for?" TJ asked.

Oz grabbed his coat and keys and headed for his door. "Your blessing, I guess."

"You can have it. But for the record, this means we're no longer even for Tajikistan."

"Duly noted."

PHOEBE HAD ENDURED several long days of overseeing the repackaging of the 'Pharaohs and Phantoms' Egyptian exhibit. She liked being back to the routine of the museum, but she also wanted to travel again soon. Amyrtaeus had said more adventures awaited her, and Phoebe had dwelled on those words for the entire trip back from Egypt.

What did it mean? What if she could find other artifacts with ghosts linked to them—ghosts who could lead her to more long-lost discoveries?

Back in her office, she packed up her briefcase, still lost in thought. She could take intermittent expeditions, like the Egyptian one. Since she credited her museum with the discovery she'd made in Egypt, with Tremaine's permission, of course, her museum had received a token of the fame, too. She felt certain she could convince the museum's board of directors to let her take a few more trips like that every year, to boost the museum's exposure.

But part of the enjoyment of the Egypt expedition had been undertaking it with Oz. Would he be willing to take more trips with her—as her protection? Or would he see through her ruse, knowing it was just an effort to try to spend more time with him? No. No ruse. When the work of the Egyptian exhibit was finished, she'd call Oz and ask him if he wanted to come for a visit.

"Phoebe?"

She spun around to see Oz standing in the doorway. He wore blue jeans and a faded blue t-shirt. His dark hair was neatly combed, and he had several days of stubble on his jaw.

She smiled. "Oz!"

Ozymandias stepped into her office and dropped his jacket on one of the chairs. "Do you know that your smile lights up my world?"

Blushing, she took a step closer to him. "I do now."

He placed his hands on her waist. "I'd like to see where we can take this relationship."

Heat coursed through her at his touch. "It could be dangerous."

"Oh? Do you have more gun-wielding ex-boyfriends on the loose?"

She wrapped her arms around his neck. "No, but I *was* thinking we could find the next spirit willing to help us uncover a great new discovery."

His eyes sparkled. "Were you now?"

"We make a good team."

"We make an excellent team, and I'd love to take the next adventure with you." He reached into his pocket and pulled out two stones.

Phoebe stepped back with a gasp. "You got the gems! How?"

"I took them with me when the lights went out in that tomb. I wanted to make sure you got what you deserved. Amyrtaeus would have wanted you to have these, right?" Oz raised his hand, offering the gemstones to her.

Phoebe picked up the emerald. "He would have wanted *us* to have these. You keep the ruby, and the two stones will keep us connected wherever we go."

"In life and in death?"

She looked into his eyes. Oz appeared amused with the idea rather than frightened by it. "Ozymandias Levine—

King of Kings, King of Air. I'm going to kiss you now, and I'm not going to apologize for it."

She leaned in and touched her lips to his. Their warmth and passion overtook her as he wrapped his arms around her and pressed his body against hers. She lost herself in his warm embrace.

<<<<THE END>>>>

~

****QUICK NOTE FROM THE AUTHOR****

IF YOU ENJOYED Phoebe's Pharaoh, I hope you'll sign up for my newsletter if you haven't already to learn more about the Romancing the Spirit Series. Keep reading for a sneak preview of the next in the series.

Romancing the Spirit

IN BOXED SETS

INDIVIDUAL BOOKS
  Romancing the Spirit Series #1
  Sadie's Spirit / Willow's Windfall
  Cassie's Chase / Phoebe's Pharaoh

Vanessa's Valentine / Autumn's Angel
Romancing the Spirit Series #2
Carol's Christmas / Allison's Alibi
Gracelynn's Genie / Michelle's Miracle
Heather's Hero / Chloe's Cupid
Romancing the Spirit Series #3
Sabrina's Storm / Jenny's Justice
Stella's Star / Gigi's Gift
Phoenix's Phantom / Fiona's Freedom

THE CHRISTMAS COLLECTION

DEAR READER

If you enjoyed this book and want to know about future releases by CB Samet, you can CLICK HERE to sign up for my mailing list! I promise I won't spam you. I only send an email when I have a new book released, give-aways, or special discounts. And I'll never sell your information. You can also unsubscribe at any time.

Also, as an independent author, I rely heavily on readers to spread the word about books they've read. If you enjoyed this story, kindly let others know by posing a brief comment on social media or leave a review where you purchased it.

Thank you for reading,

CB Samet

OTHER BOOKS BY CB SAMET

Looking for more romantic suspense? How about with an urban fantasy twist? More heat, more action.

Check out The Shadow Guardians trilogy.

Get *Raven's Flight, a prequel novella* for FREE. In my newsletter, you'll learn about me, special discounts, and new releases.

Olympian Awakenings Trilogy

Urban fantasy Greek Mythology Adventure

Grab the prequel exclusively HERE.

Stone Hearts

Winds of Destiny

Flame and Shadow

The Dr. Whyte Adventure Novels
Thriller Series

Black Gold

Whyte Knight

Gray Horizon

Love action/adventure and strong female leads in a fantasy world? Check out my other genre:

The Avant Champion Fantasy Series

The Avant Champion: Rising

Malakai: An Avant Champion Origin of Malos Story (prequel)

The Avant Champion: Honor

The Avant Champion: Ashes

Brothers' Bond: An Avant Champion Malakai Story

The Avant Champion: Conquest

Isabel: An Avant Champion novelette

The Avant Champion: Redeem

VANESSA'S VALENTINE - SAMPLE

An undercover DEA agent on the run. A sinister drug smuggler with a vengeance. And Vanessa is caught between them.

Rural physician, Vanessa Watson, escaped the bustling urban ER for a slower pace and more personalized patient care. But when a mysterious stranger climbs into Vanessa's car, bullets start flying. Vanessa saves Seth from imminent danger, but the act of saving a life puts her own in danger.

Five years of undercover work are blown in an instant, and Seth Dellosa loses his partner, Rico, and his identity. On the run for his life, he seeks shelter from his enemies in Vanessa's home. With the help of his deceased partner's ghost, Seth faces the pressure to bring down the drug cartel before they find him and the innocent woman aiding him.

But the Mexican drug smuggler who Seth deceived is out for blood and determined to find the traitor who infiltrated his organization.

SAMPLE CHAPTER ONE

Vanessa stepped out into the cool February night, carrying her medical bag in one hand and a dozen roses in the other. The balance was precarious as she tried to hug the heavy, rose-laden vase close to her body, while at the same time not get impaled by the gazillion tiny thorns along the stems of the beautiful flowers.

Where in her minuscule house was she going to put this ostentatious, gargantuan bouquet?

She slipped the straps of her medical bag up high on her forearm and freed one hand in order to open the door of her electric blue Ford Fiesta. She carefully positioned the vase in the passenger seat, cushioning it with her medical bag so it wouldn't fall forward.

After closing the door, she walked around the front of the car and sank into the driver's seat. Outside, the sun had nearly set, and the clinic parking lot sat vacant. A single floodlight lit the small brick building.

Just as she pushed the START button on her car, the door behind her opened. The car jolted as someone landed in the back seat—before slamming the door shut behind them.

"Drive!" a male voice commanded.

Jumping in her seat, Vanessa looked into the rearview mirror to find a bearded man in a sweatsuit half-sitting, half-slouching in the back seat.

"Get out of my car!" she screamed, heart rate spiking with fear.

A loud crack coincided with the shattering of her back window.

She ducked lower in her seat. "Is someone *shooting* at you?"

"Drive!" the intruder barked again.

This time, Vanessa slammed her car into drive and peeled out of the parking lot. She sped north on the highway, the engine of her small car whining in protest.

She glanced in the rearview mirror to see a pickup truck tailing them. Gripping the wheel tightly as adrenaline surged through her body, she embraced her flight mode.

"What the hell is going on?" she demanded.

"Those men work for Julio Oquiñena. He's a Mexican drug dealer."

"And *you* are?"

"My name is Seth Dellosa. I'm an undercover DEA agent." Seth winced as she swerved to avoid a pothole.

"I'm supposed to believe you?"

"I'm hoping the truth will motivate you to help me."

"If they're shooting at you, I'd guess you're not so undercover anymore." Her voice was harsh with the strain of keeping her composure during the car chase.

Seth snorted. "Yeah, I *was* undercover."

"Are you armed?"

"No."

Vanessa couldn't decide if this stranger being unarmed gave her more comfort or less. She glanced in the rearview mirror. "They're still following us."

"Can you lose them?"

Her heart thumped wildly against her rib cage as she navigated the back roads at a terrifying velocity. Fortunately, part of her family medicine practice involved making house calls, so she knew these roads as well as she knew every organ in the human body.

When she looked down at Seth through the rearview mirror, she noticed streaks of blood on her tan, partial leather seat.

:You're injured."

"Very astute of you, Dr. Watson."

A chill spread through Vanessa—one that competed with the heat from the fear coursing through her. "How do you know who I am?"

She'd just walked out of her own clinic and this *was* small town Texas—yet something about him knowing her name and identity spooked her. Had he been waiting in the parking lot for her, specifically? For Dr. Vanessa Watson?

"Right now, that's not important," the DEA agent insisted. "What's important is that you get us away from Julio's men."

She slammed on the brakes and made a sharp right turn onto a narrow road. The roses and vase tumbled onto the passenger side floor of the car.

In the backseat, Seth groaned.

She navigated the road with its many potholes expertly. She could tell by the erratic headlights behind her that the pickup truck was hitting most of those potholes with the ferocity of a game of Whack-a-Mole. Since their pursuers couldn't maintain their high speeds *and* navigate the numerous road hazards, the distance between the two vehicles started to lengthen.

Fifty feet before the road morphed into a wider, two-lane highway, she cut off her headlights. She made a sharp turn left and accelerated.

After several twists and turns on the dark road, she clicked on her headlights again. She couldn't continue to drive in the dark and risk hitting a deer or a bobcat. Still, she no longer saw headlights behind them.

Taking slow, steady breaths, she tried to ease her body out of flight mode. She'd never been shot at before, and her tight grip had likely made imprints on her steering wheel. She'd never been in a high-speed car chase before, either—and she'd certainly never had a man claiming to be a DEA agent bleeding in the backseat of her car.

Vanessa thought about where she was on these rural Texas back roads and began calculating their proximity to the nearest hospital—which wasn't quite so near. "I'll take you to Corpus Christi Hospital."

"No," Seth barked.

"I don't know the extent of your injuries," Vanessa shot back, "but at first glance it looks like you're bleeding, pale, and dehydrated. You need a hospital."

"I came to you for help precisely because it's not *safe* for me to go to a hospital. Julio would be able to find me in a hospital."

Vanessa clenched her jaw. It wasn't safe for her to do anything *other* than take him to a hospital. If she delivered this injured agent to a qualified medical facility, he could at least receive police protection—if he truly was the DEA agent he claimed to be.

Seth's words echoed in her mind. *I came to you for help.* The tone of his voice and the sincerity of that statement had been partially pleading.

No, no, no.

Helping this man outside of a controlled medical environment was *not* a good idea.

Vanessa gripped the wheel tighter to steel her resolve. "Look—I'm really not into getting shot at,or whatever other maiming those men have in mind. If they did that to *you*, I'm sure they'll have no compunction about killing *me*. We're going to a hospital."

Seth didn't reply.

She turned and looked in the backseat, where the bleeding DEA agent lay. He was unconscious, but his chest rose and fell, and she could see the soft pulsation of his carotid artery.

Vanessa swore. She couldn't let him die in the backseat of her car on the way to the hospital. She needed to give him emergency medical care right now.

Seth's leg throbbed as the car came to a stop with the sound of crunching gravel. The door opened, and Vanessa Watson tugged him upright. Her long red hair fell in loose ringlets over her shoulders. So close to her, he noticed a small cluster of freckles trailing across her nose.

"Looks like a gunshot wound to your leg. Do you have any other major injuries?"

"Where are we?" Seth asked.

"*La casa del doctora*," Rico told him. "She didn't take you to *el hospital*. I told you—you can trust her."

"Um. Safehouse," Vanessa replied.

"*Ella vive sola?*" Seth asked Rico. Vanessa wouldn't be able to hear Rico Valez's response. Rico was a ghost—and very few people could hear or see ghosts.

"*Sí*," Rico replied.

Vanessa helped Seth to his feet. "You should know my Spanish is a work in progress … if you're going to insist on going back and forth between English and Spanish."

"*Es este lugar seguro?*" Seth asked Rico.

"*Sí. Solamente un perro.*"

"Great. You're delirious." Vanessa sighed.

Seth's former partner, Rico, hovered beside him—a translucent shadow of his former self. Rico followed as the doctor assisted Seth, moving him toward her house and helping him keep most of his weight on his right—uninjured—leg. With every excruciating step, Seth felt like someone was driving a knife into his thigh.

Vanessa's house was a small, ancient-looking wood cabin with a tiny, rickety porch. In the dim evening light, Seth could make out trees along the boundary of what appeared to be about ten acres or so of ungrazed pasture-land. Seth eyed the black Labrador standing on the porch, greeting them with a robustly wagging tail.

"Don't worry about Crick, he's friendly," Vanessa promised.

Seth struggled up the steps, taking them one at a time while simultaneously trying not to crush Vanessa with his weight, or pass out from the pain. Fresh, hot blood oozed from his leg as a cold sweat trickled down his neck.

As if sensing his escalating duress, Vanessa situated herself closer to support him. Seth's nostrils flared as they filled with the scent of her—a combination of roses and honey laced with vanilla. He recalled the roses she'd carried out from her clinic and put in her car. Immediately following that moment, he'd made the decision to climb into her vehicle, dragging her into the danger in his life.

Vanessa managed to unlock the front door while still supporting him. As they entered, she flicked on the light switch. The couch caught his eye, enticing him to lie down and close his eyes.

"Oh no, you don't." She steered him toward her kitchen.

"The kitchen?"

"Oh, we're back to English now?" She helped him onto the counter, where she made Seth lay flat and stretch out his leg.

The hard, uncomfortable surface was the least part of his discomfort. She placed a pillow from the sofa under his head. He felt consciousness slipping away from him.

Then, he felt her gloved hands on him—cutting clothes and inspecting his injuries. She spoke as she worked, explaining her every move in a soothing voice.

Seth's eyes grew heavy until they closed altogether.

Vanessa worked quickly, flashing back to her year of emergency medicine training. She'd left that career path behind her, but with Seth's injuries before her, she was instantly reminded of the intense pressure and rush of working under a ticking clock on a trauma patient.

She opened her physician bag and lined up her equipment: forceps, bandages, lidocaine and syringe, disinfectant, and suture thread with needle. She cut off Seth's sweatshirt and placed a wristband and electrodes on his exposed skin. The electrodes transmitted wirelessly to the wristband, displaying his electrocardiogram rhythm. The wristband tracked his heart rate and oxygen levels. So far, his vital signs didn't indicate hemorrhagic shock.

With the man's pants now converted to shorts, she applied a pressure dressing to his leg. She'd have to come back to that wound, which had dark venous blood emerging from it—not the bright, brisk arterial blood.

With a handheld ultrasound, she checked his vital organs for damage. There were no collapsed lungs, no blood around his heart, and no hemorrhage in his abdomen. When she finished her assessment, Vanessa inventoried his injuries: a gunshot wound to the leg, which appeared to be through and through the muscle, plus a laceration to his right forearm needing stitches, and a host of superficial bruising. Seth had taken a beating before or after taking the bullet.

She looked at the sleeping stranger. His beard extended longer than the dark, sweaty hair plastered to his head. She'd cut off his shirt and most of his sweatpants. His toned body boasted defined musculature, but wasn't bulky. He had no track marks and good dentition, so while it remained to be seen whether he was friend or foe, he wasn't a junkie. That would make him easier to sedate. Considering the work she still needed to do—not to mention the pain it would induce—Vanessa didn't want a startled, disoriented patient waking and lashing out at her.

She started an IV and hung a bag of saline. Then, she roused Seth and helped him take oral narcotics to keep him comfortable. When he lay back once again, he closed his eyes. She watched his vital signs as she disinfected, anesthetized tissue, sutured, and bandaged.

Crick, who'd been quietly lying on his rug watching her, whined.

"Right, food. Sorry, boy." Vanessa broke away from doctoring to feed the hungry Lab.

After she took care of Crick, Vanessa removed Seth's cowboy boots. She took his wallet from his back pocket, opened it, and stared at the driver's license within.

"Jorge Hernandez, huh?"

She looked again at the dozing, half-naked man on her kitchen counter. Despite the paleness of his skin from the blood loss, Seth had a clearly dark complexion— suggesting potentially Hispanic origins. His Spanish sounded beautifully melodic, too—yet his English had been crisp, without a Spanish accent.

Vanessa needed to get Seth—or Jorge, or whoever this man was—off her countertop. She had a bed or a couch to offer, but the couch was too short for him.

With the liter of fluid almost out, she removed his IV. She hadn't given Seth a comatose level of narcotics, so he should be able to help her move himself.

Here goes nothing.

Vanessa slid an arm underneath him and began to pull the big man upright. "Seth, I need you to wake up and help me move you."

When he stirred and sat up, she helped him swing his legs off the edge of the countertop. Because he didn't grimace, she suspected the combination of local anesthetic and systemic narcotics had sufficiently blunted the pain of his gunshot wound. Fortunately, the bullet hadn't lodged in his leg, so she'd only had to patch him up and not dig around for a foreign object.

"Rico, donde estoy?"

"Oh, I know that one. You want to know where you are. You're at my house. I don't know who Rico is, though. I'm Dr. Watson."

Seth's green eyes focused on her. He reached out his hands and cupped her face. "You are so beautiful."

She gave a nervous chuckle as she dodged his gaze. She positioned herself beside him to help Seth down off the counter.

"That's the drugs talking. I may have been a little generous with the meds as a precaution, for my own safety. You know, I once had a patient tell me he'd give me his gizzard while he was under the influence of benzodiazepines and narcotics. Being a city girl, I had to look up what the heck a gizzard was."

Seth smiled at her, maintaining his intense gaze. "Your hair is amazing. Like a rippling sunset."

"Well, it's winter. You should see this red mane in the Texas heat and humidity. I look like an alpaca. They really should put a warning label on this state for people with long hair thinking of moving here."

He chuckled and seemed unfazed about continuing to stare at Vanessa as if she was a movie star.

"Down you go. Watch the weight on your left leg.

You're all patched up, but don't strain anything. I hope your tetanus shot is up to date." She kept those in her office, not at her home.

Vanessa helped Seth through her living room and into her bedroom. When she tried to ease him onto her bed, his weight was too much for her and she was pulled down with him. She drew up her leg, trying not to bump his wound but ended up just straddling him on the bed.

His hands slid along her waist. Her breath hitched at the smooth sensuality of his touch. His calloused palms felt both tantalizing and tender.

"Vanessa." He pulled her closer and pressed his lips to her neck.

The feel of his bare chest, hard body, and hot breath sent heated desire through Vanessa's body.

Impossible.

Logical thought prevailed over hormones as she pushed herself up and off of him. For heaven's sake—she didn't even know this man!

But Seth smiled knowingly, as though aware she'd pushed away despite the sparks flying between them. Seeing that he knew the effect he'd had on her, even if only for a moment, hardened Vanessa's resolve. She began to move further away, but hesitated when Seth's dark green eyes looked at her with something like adoration. Then, she saw his constricted pupils, reminding her that he was buzzing under the influence of the narcotics she'd given him.

"You felt amazing," Seth said in a husky rasp.

"Yes, well—you're already expressing yourself *without* words." She avoided looking at the part of him that seemed to want her the most. Getting shot and drugged didn't seem to impact his ability to become noticeably aroused.

"Thank you for helping me."

Vanessa looked down at the floor and rubbed the sole of her shoe along a zigzag design on the gray carpet. "Get some rest."

"What about you?"

"I'll be in the other room if you need anything."

He nodded. "I'm sorry for the trouble."

Vanessa wanted desperately to ask him how bad the trouble was. What danger had she exposed herself to in helping this handsome stranger? But she'd save those questions for when they were both better rested.

"Vanessa?"

"Yes."

"What day is it?"

"February fourteenth. Valentine's Day." Vanessa pulled the door to her bedroom shut as she left.

<<<CONTINUE READING HERE>>>

www.ingramcontent.com/pod-product-compliance
Lightning Source LLC
Chambersburg PA
CBHW030315130626
46549CB00002B/867